Disney
Tangled
The Series

The Friendship Mix-Up

By
NEW YORK TIMES
Bestselling
author

Jimmy
Gownley

Illustrated
by

Veronica
Di Lorenzo,

Caroline
LaVelle
Egan,

Monica
Catalano,

and
Jeffrey
Thomas

Colors
by

Anastasia
Belousova

and
Chintsova Yana
Konstantinovna

Random House 🏠 New York

Lettering by Chris Dickey

Designed by Kurt Hartman

Edited by Lauren A. Burniac and Holly Rice

Managing Editor: Cathryn McHugh

Published in the United States by Random House Children's Books, a division of Penguin Random House LLC, 1745 Broadway, New York, NY 10019, and in Canada by Penguin Random House Canada Limited, Toronto, in conjunction with Disney Enterprises, Inc. Random House and the colophon are registered trademarks of Penguin Random House LLC.

rhcbooks.com

ISBN 978-0-7364-3848-3 (trade)—
ISBN 978-0-7364-9023-8 (lib. bdg.)

MANUFACTURED IN CHINA

10 9 8 7 6 5 4 3 2 1

Random House Children's Books supports the First Amendment and celebrates the right to read.

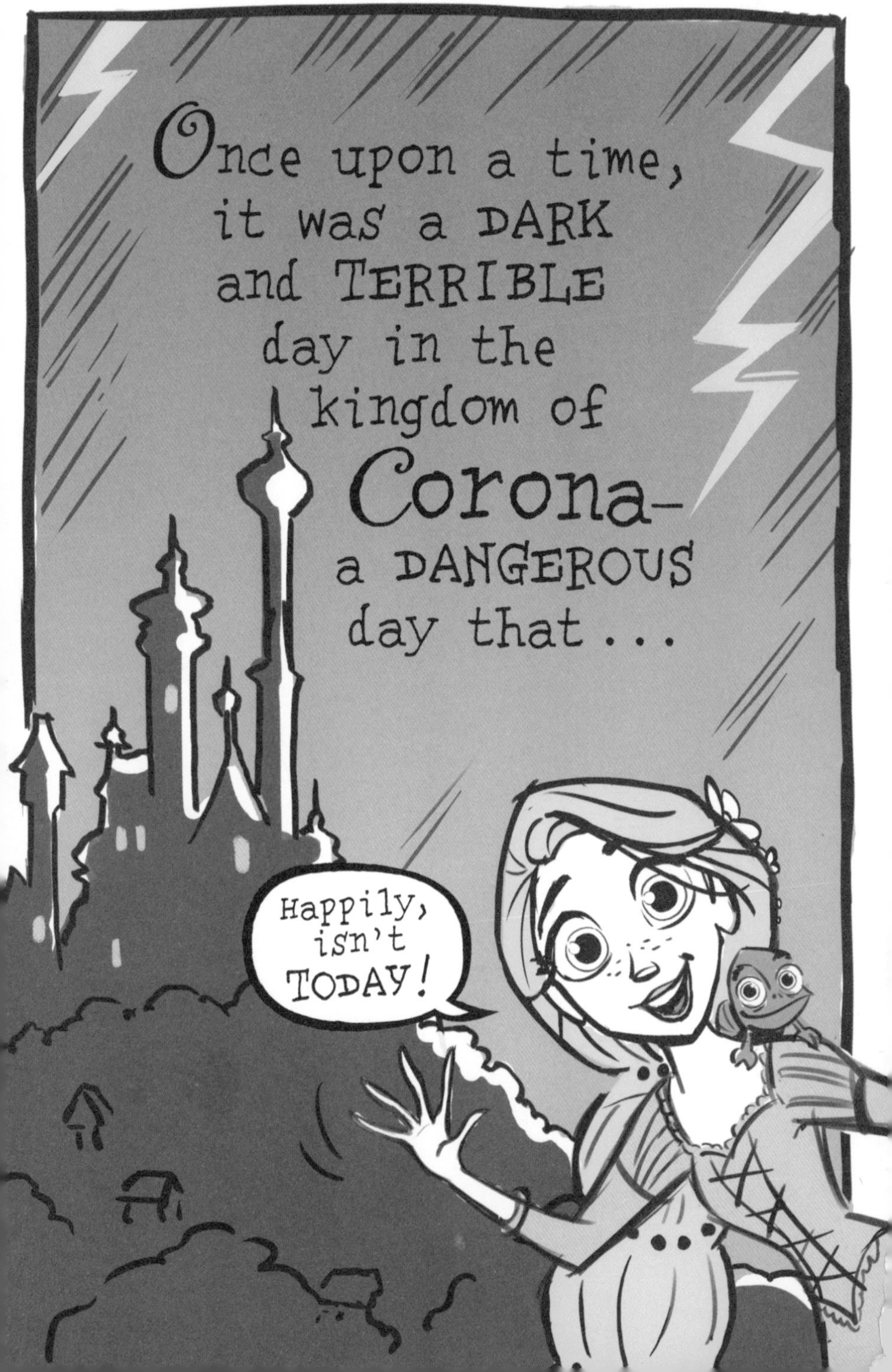
Once upon a time, it was a DARK and TERRIBLE day in the kingdom of Corona— a DANGEROUS day that . . .
Happily, isn't TODAY!

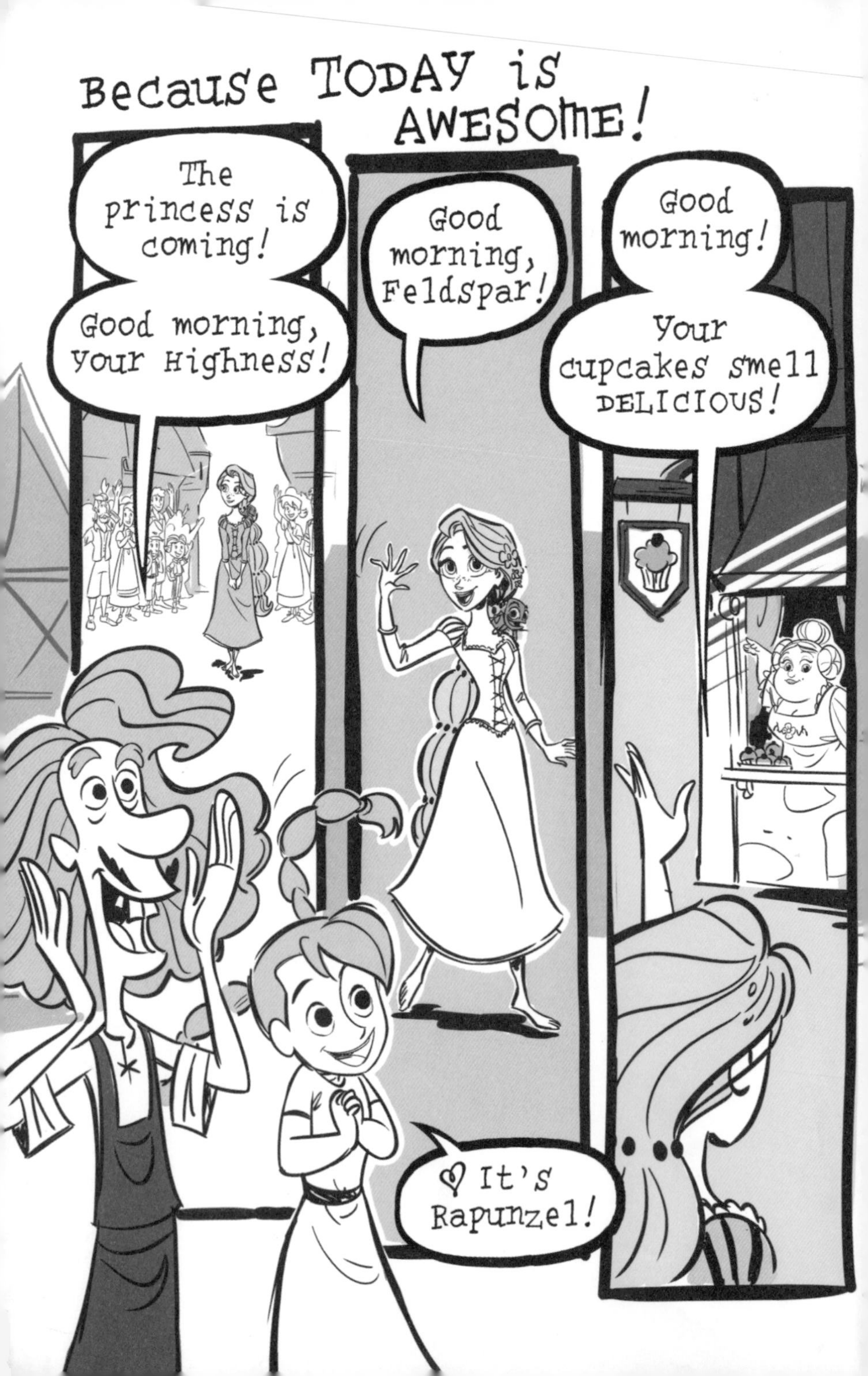

Because TODAY is AWESOME!
The princess is coming!
Good morning, your Highness!
Good morning, Feldspar!
Good morning!
Your cupcakes smell DELICIOUS!
It's Rapunzel!

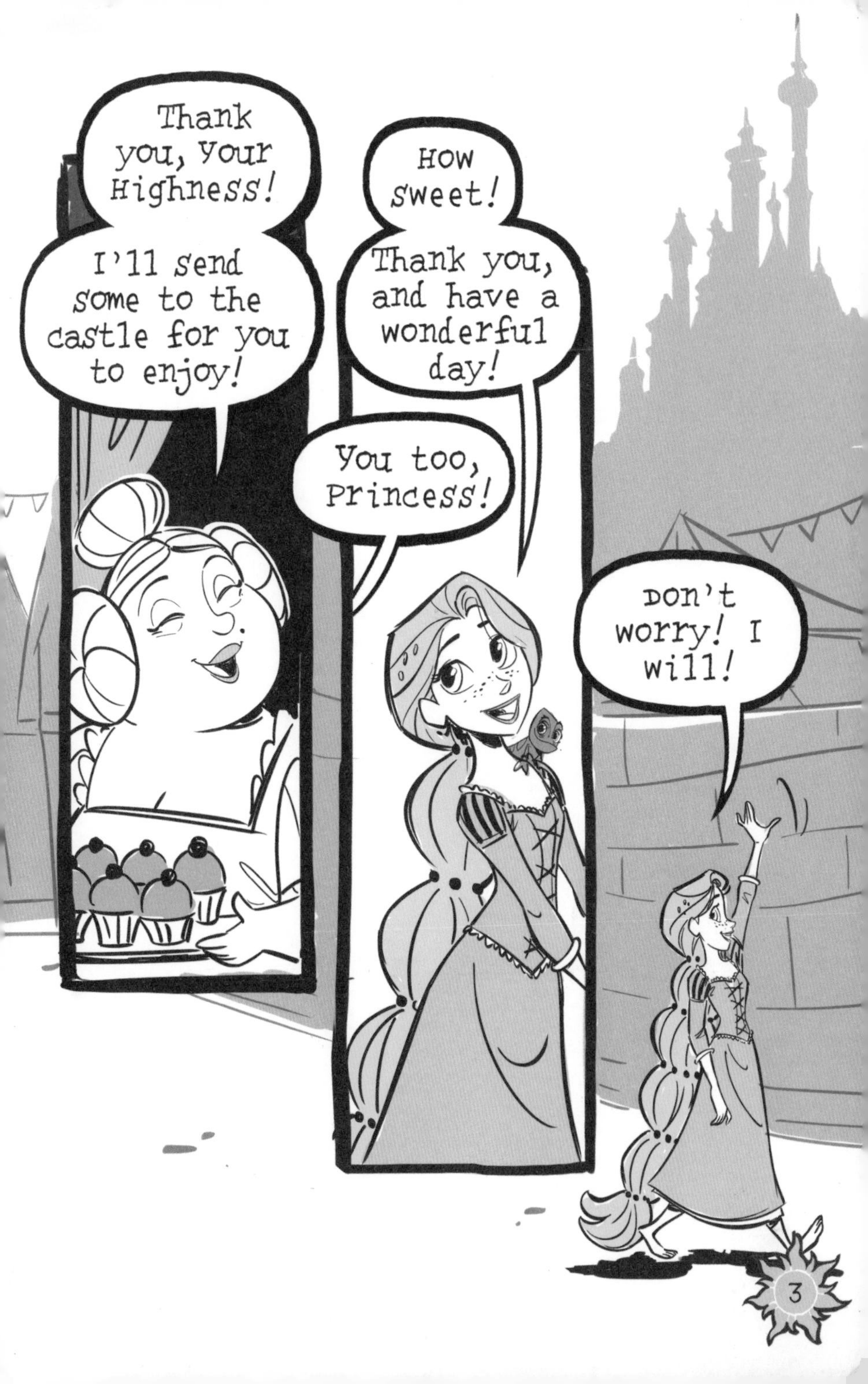
Thank you, your Highness!
I'll send some to the castle for you to enjoy!
How sweet!
Thank you, and have a wonderful day!
You too, Princess!
Don't worry! I will!

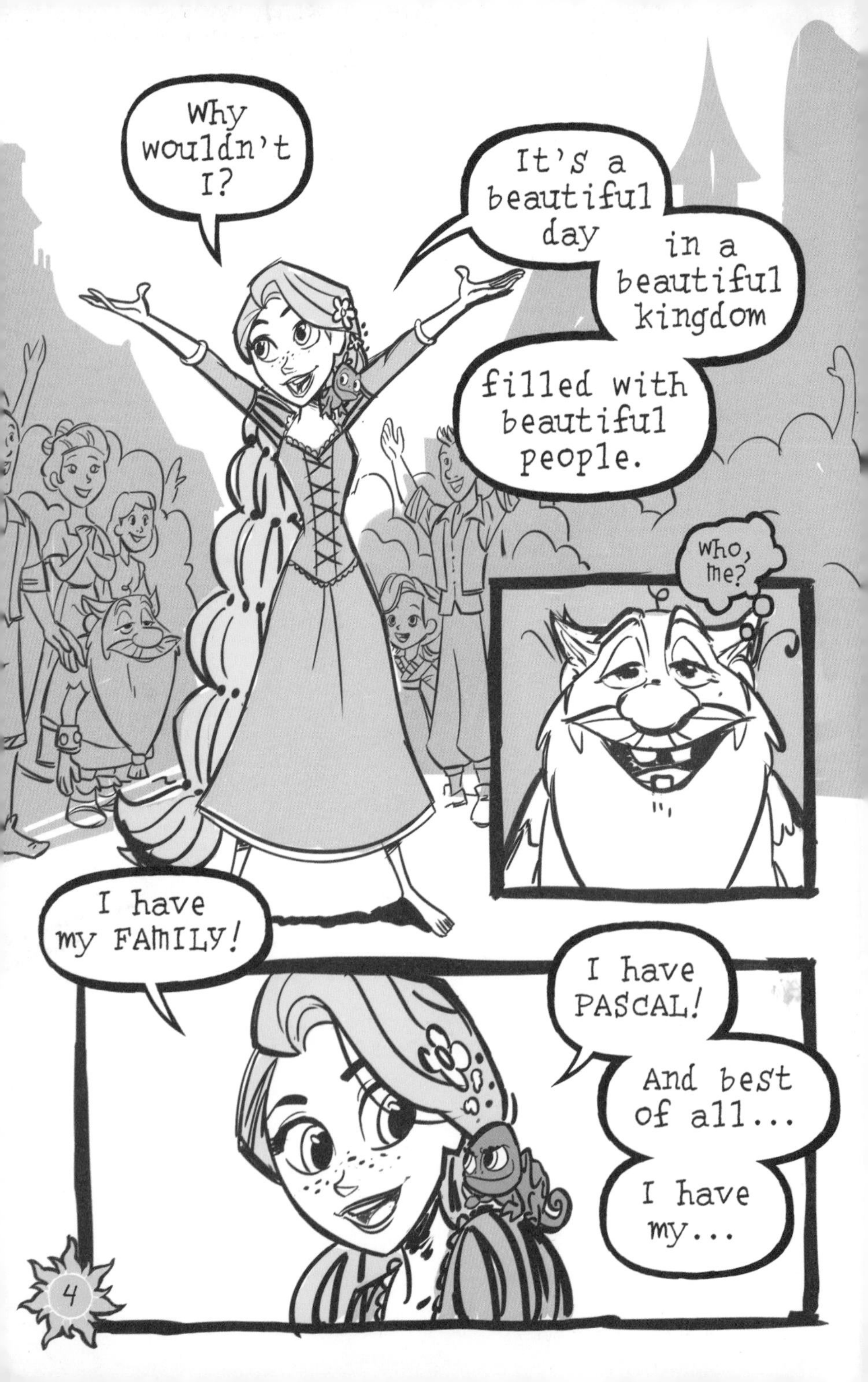
Why wouldn't I?
It's a beautiful day
in a beautiful kingdom
filled with beautiful people.
Who, me?
I have my FAMILY!
I have PASCAL!
And best of all...
I have my...

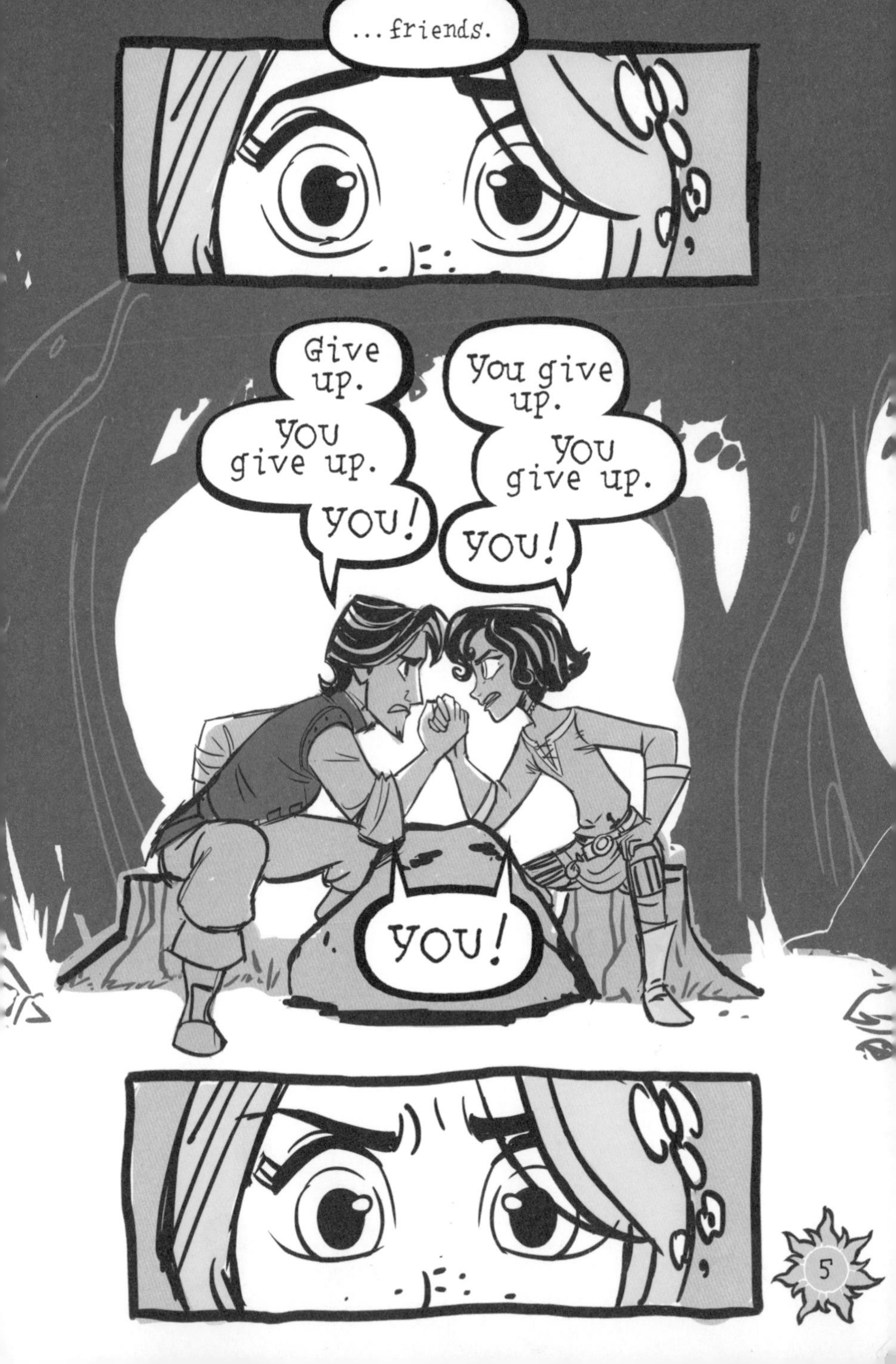
...friends.
Give up.
You give up.
YOU give up.
YOU give up.
YOU!
YOU!
YOU!

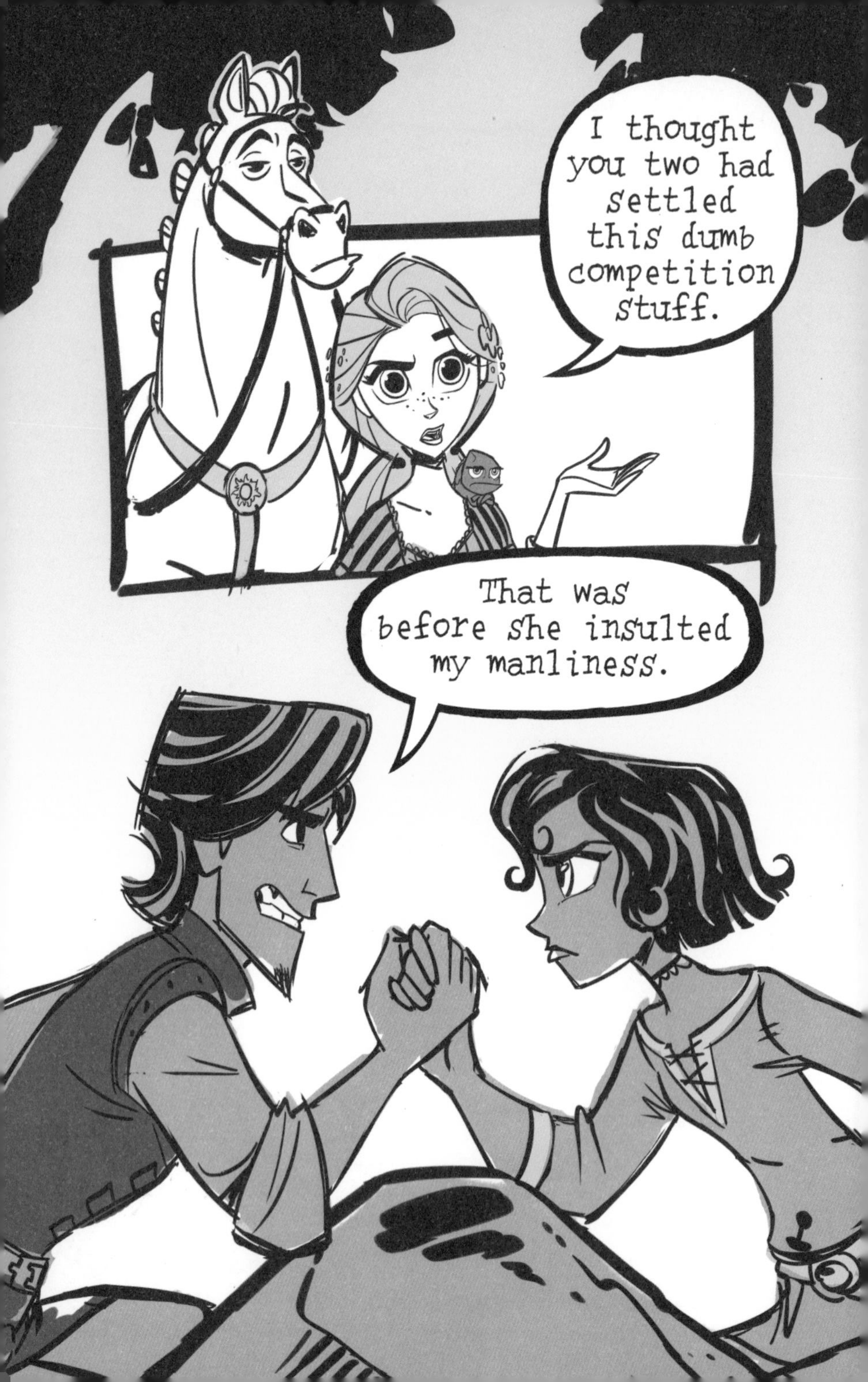
I thought you two had settled this dumb competition stuff.
That was before she insulted my manliness.

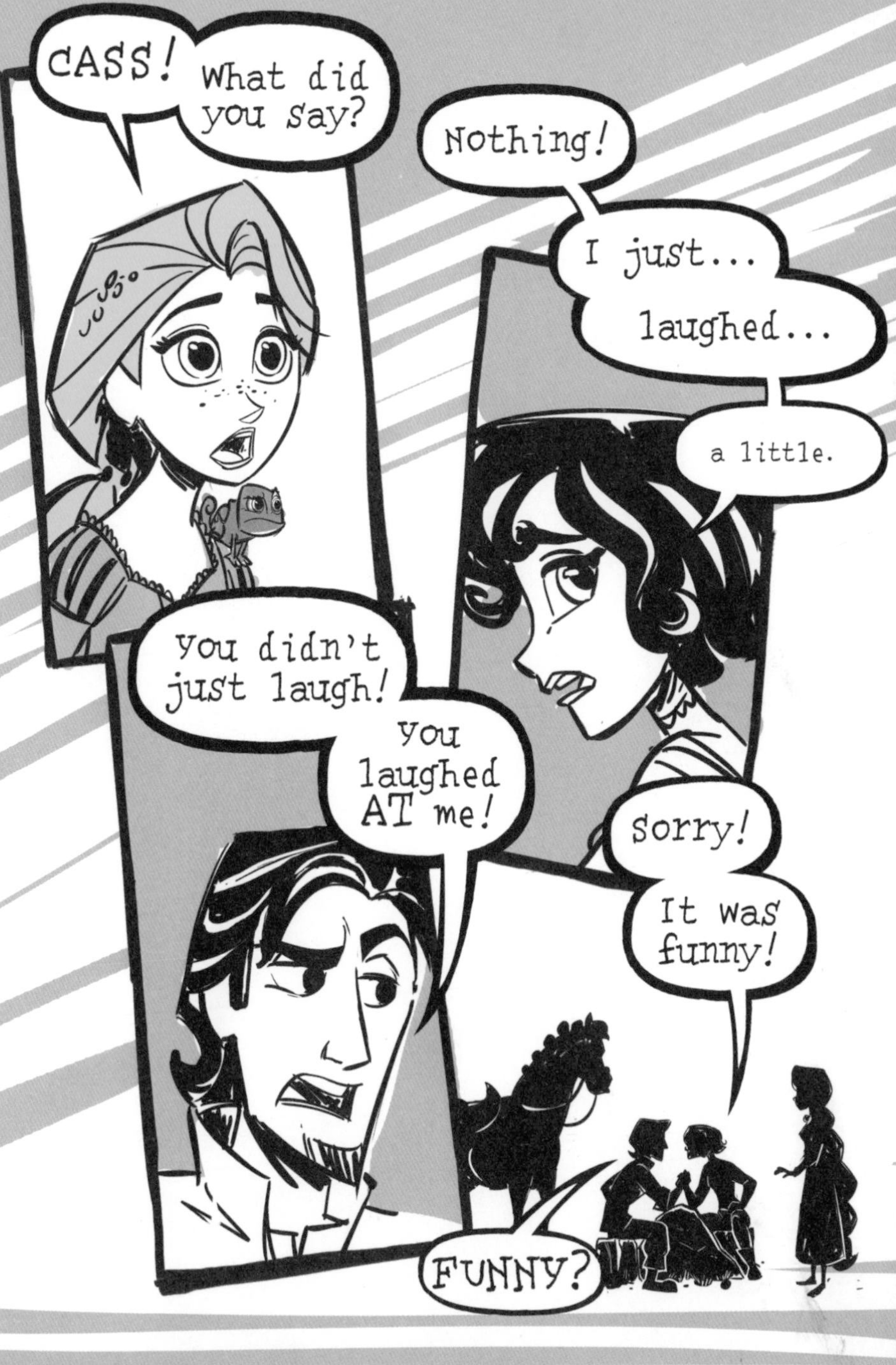
CASS!
What did you say?
Nothing!
I just...
laughed...
a little.
You didn't just laugh!
You laughed AT me!
Sorry!
It was funny!
FUNNY?

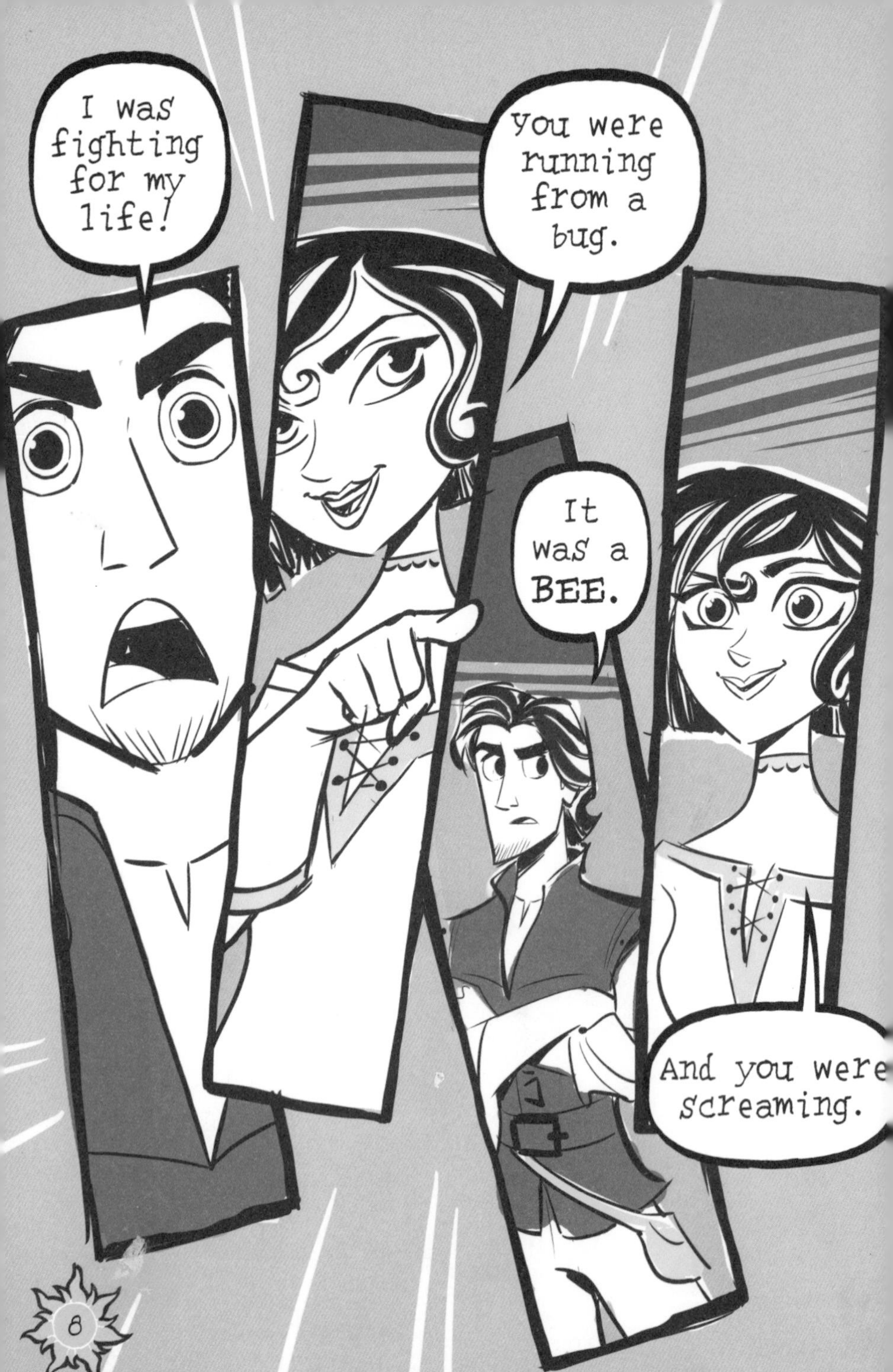
I was fighting for my life!
You were running from a bug.
It was a BEE.
And you were screaming.

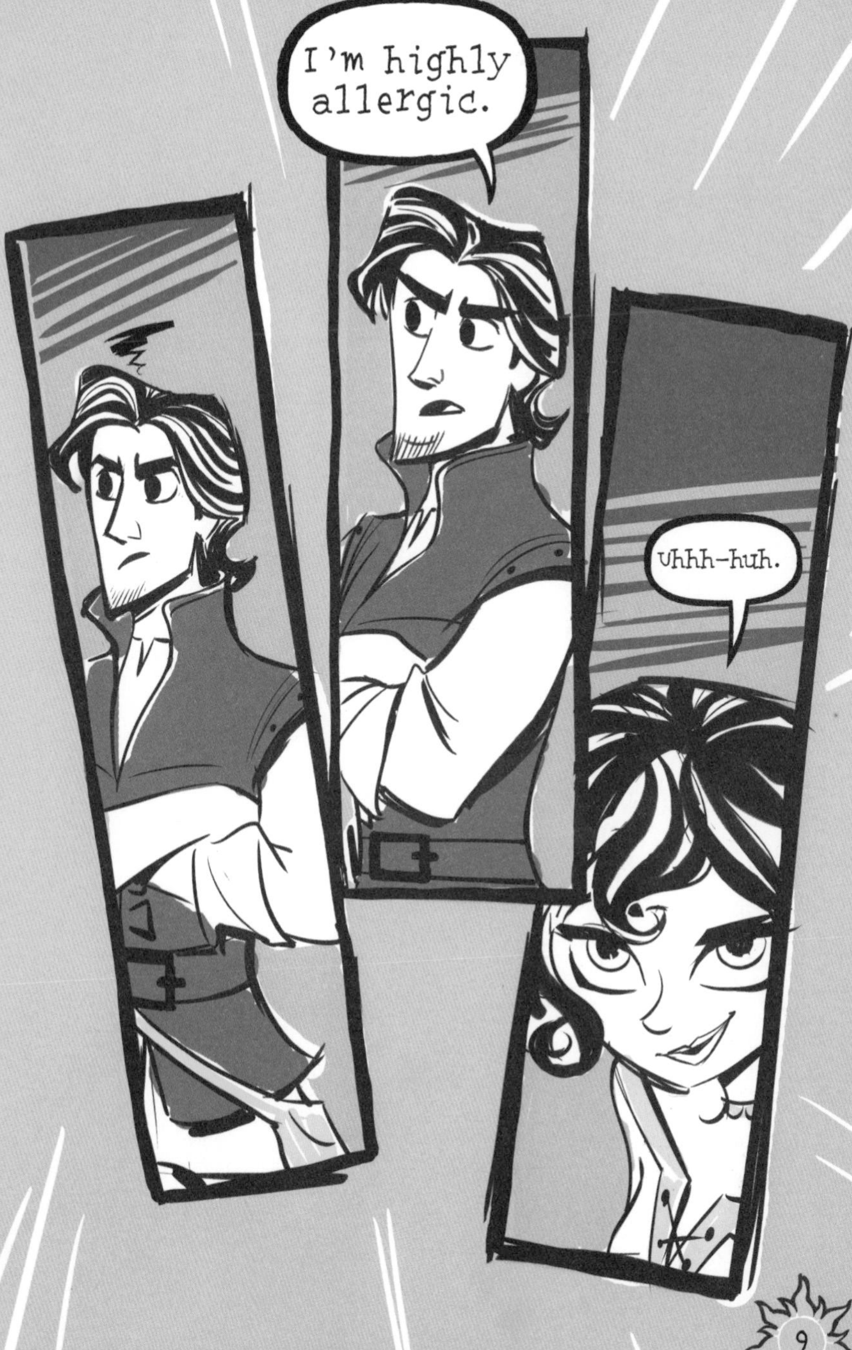
I'm highly allergic.
Uhhh-huh.

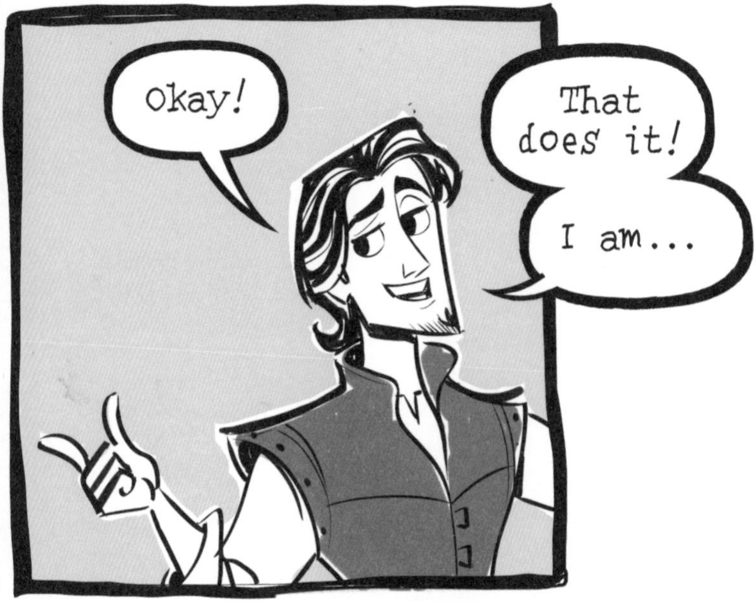
Okay!
That does it!
I am...

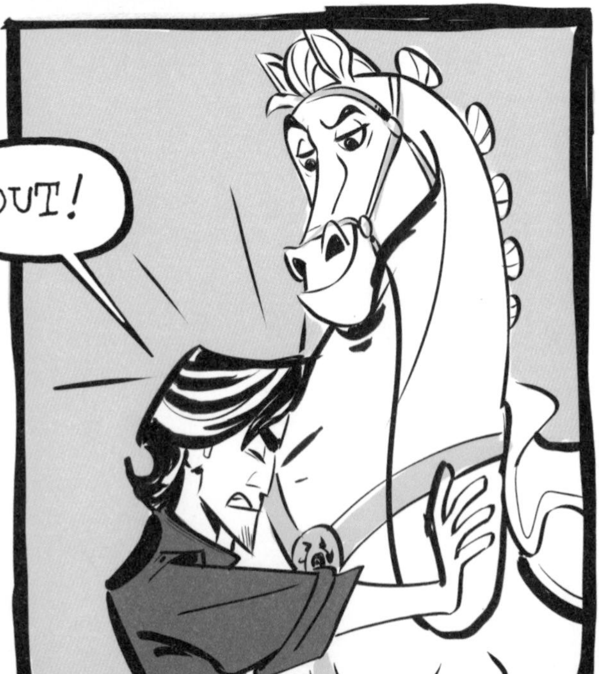
OUT!

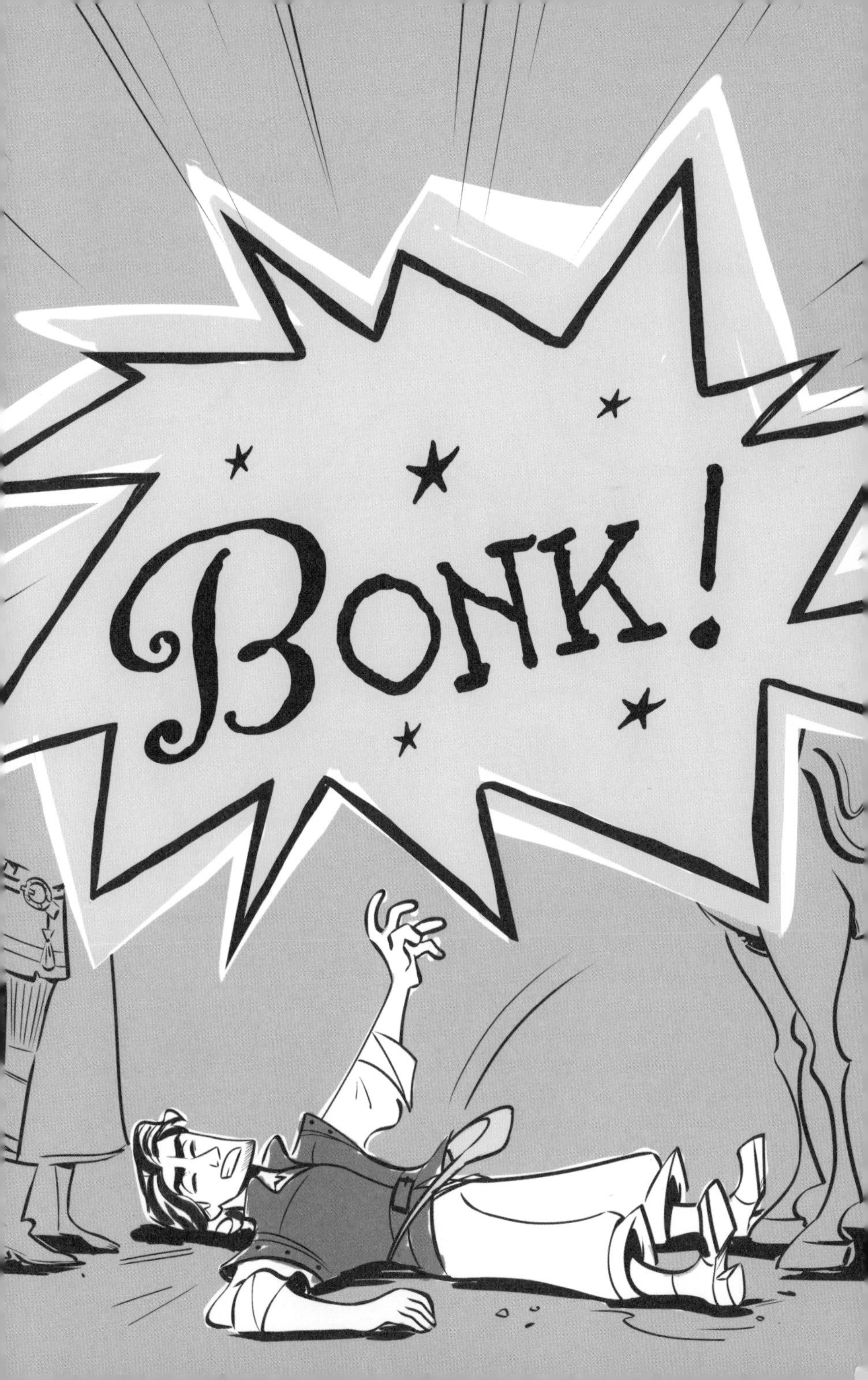
BONK!

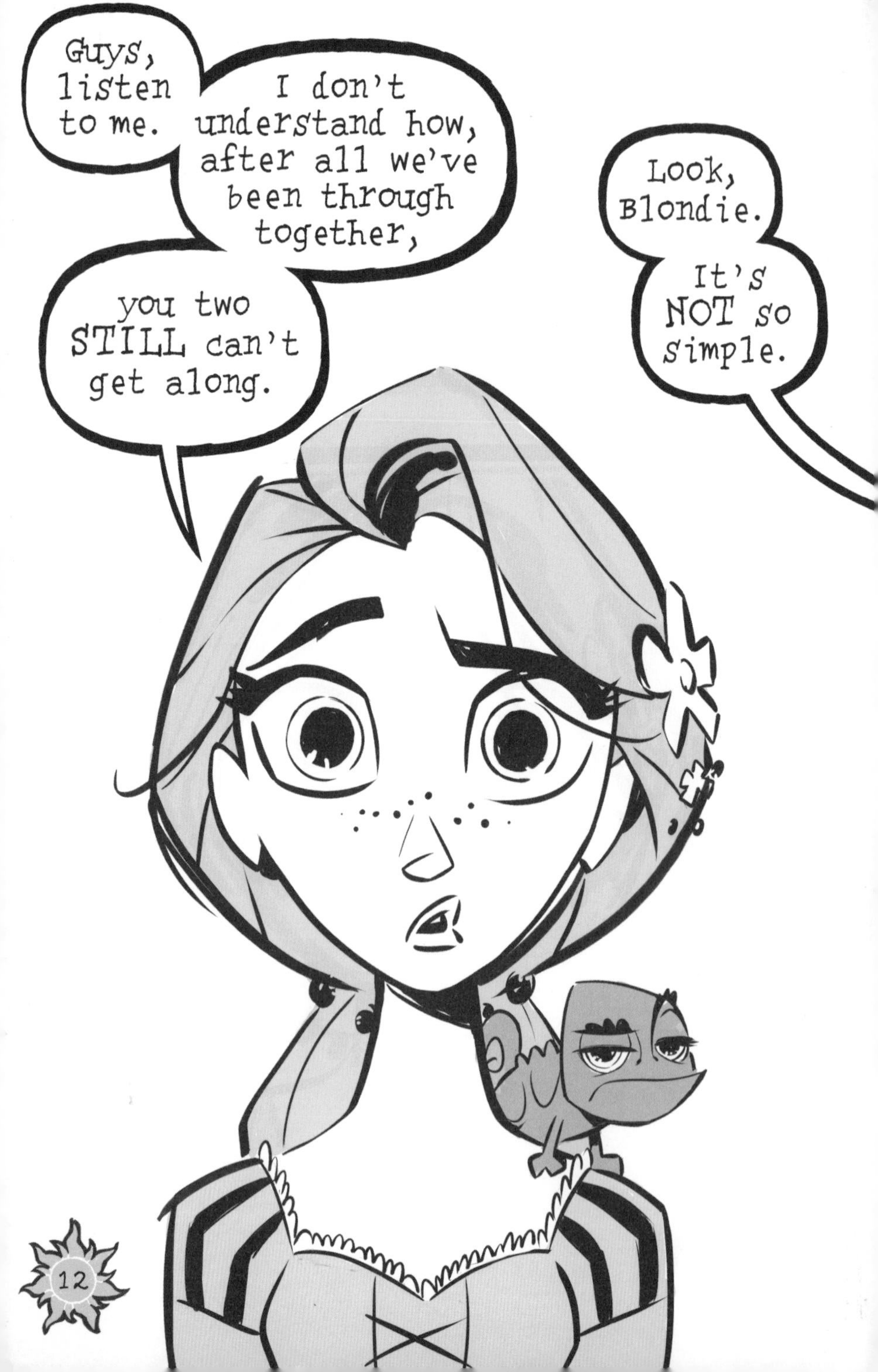
Guys, listen to me.
I don't understand how, after all we've been through together,
you two STILL can't get along.
Look, Blondie.
It's NOT so simple.

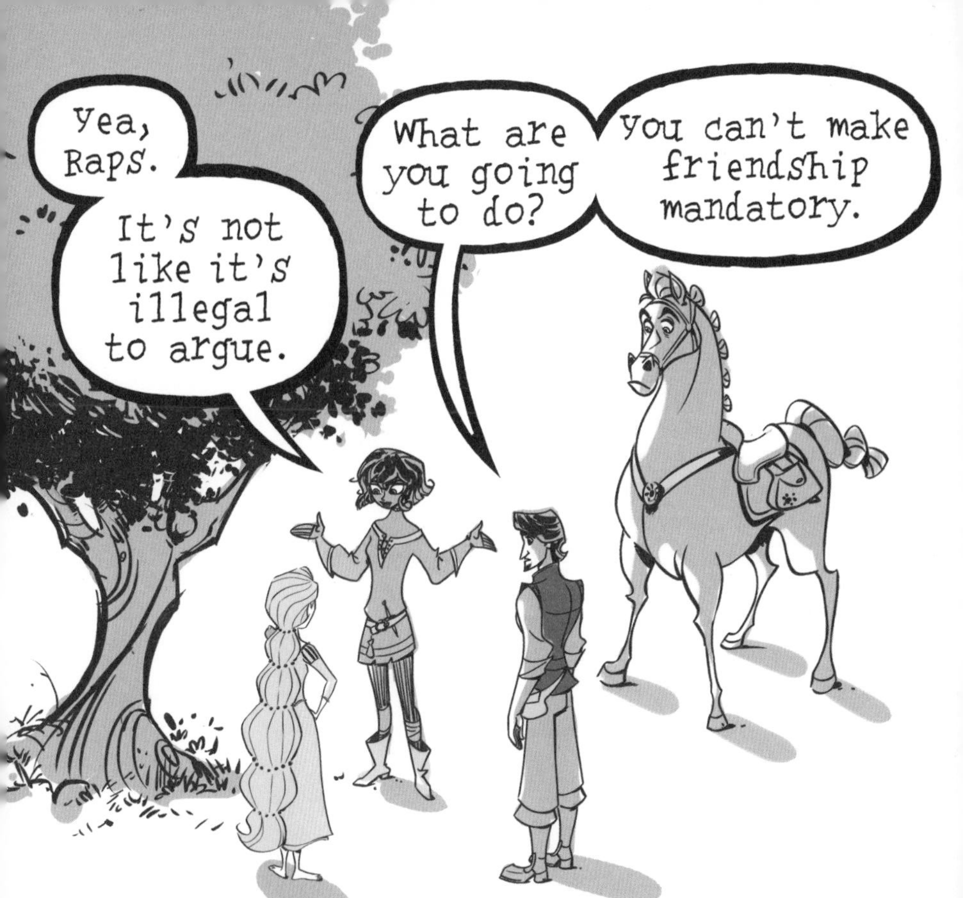
Yea, Raps.
It's not like it's illegal to argue.
What are you going to do?
You can't make friendship mandatory.

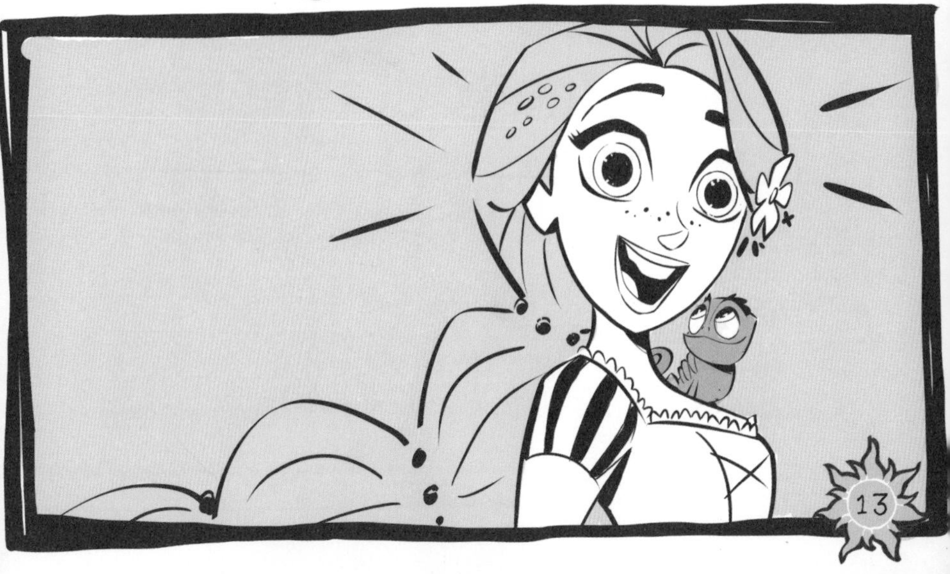

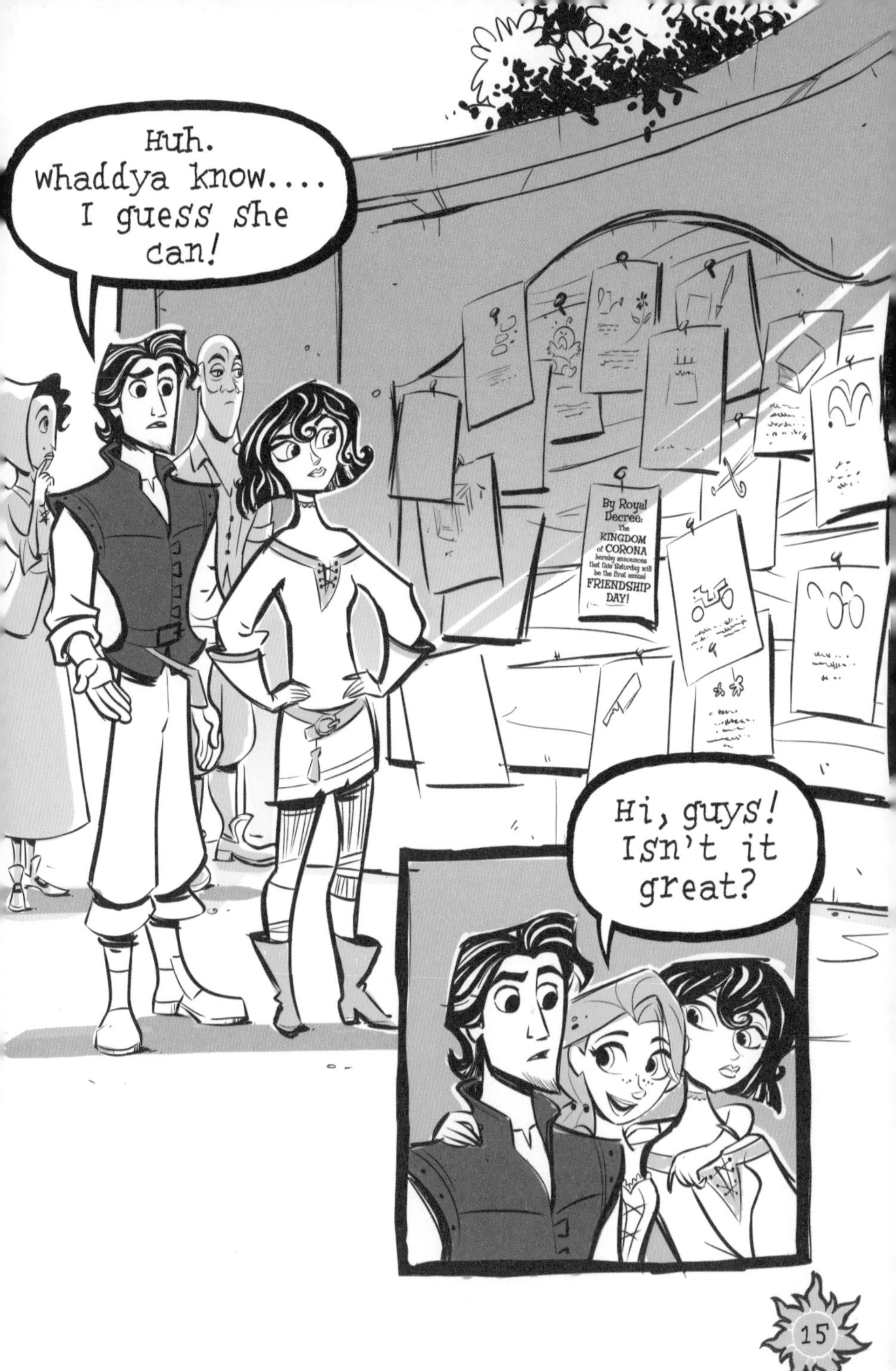
Huh. Whaddya know.... I guess she can!
By Royal Decree: The KINGDOM of CORONA hereby announces that this Saturday will be the first annual FRIENDSHIP DAY!
Hi, guys! Isn't it great?

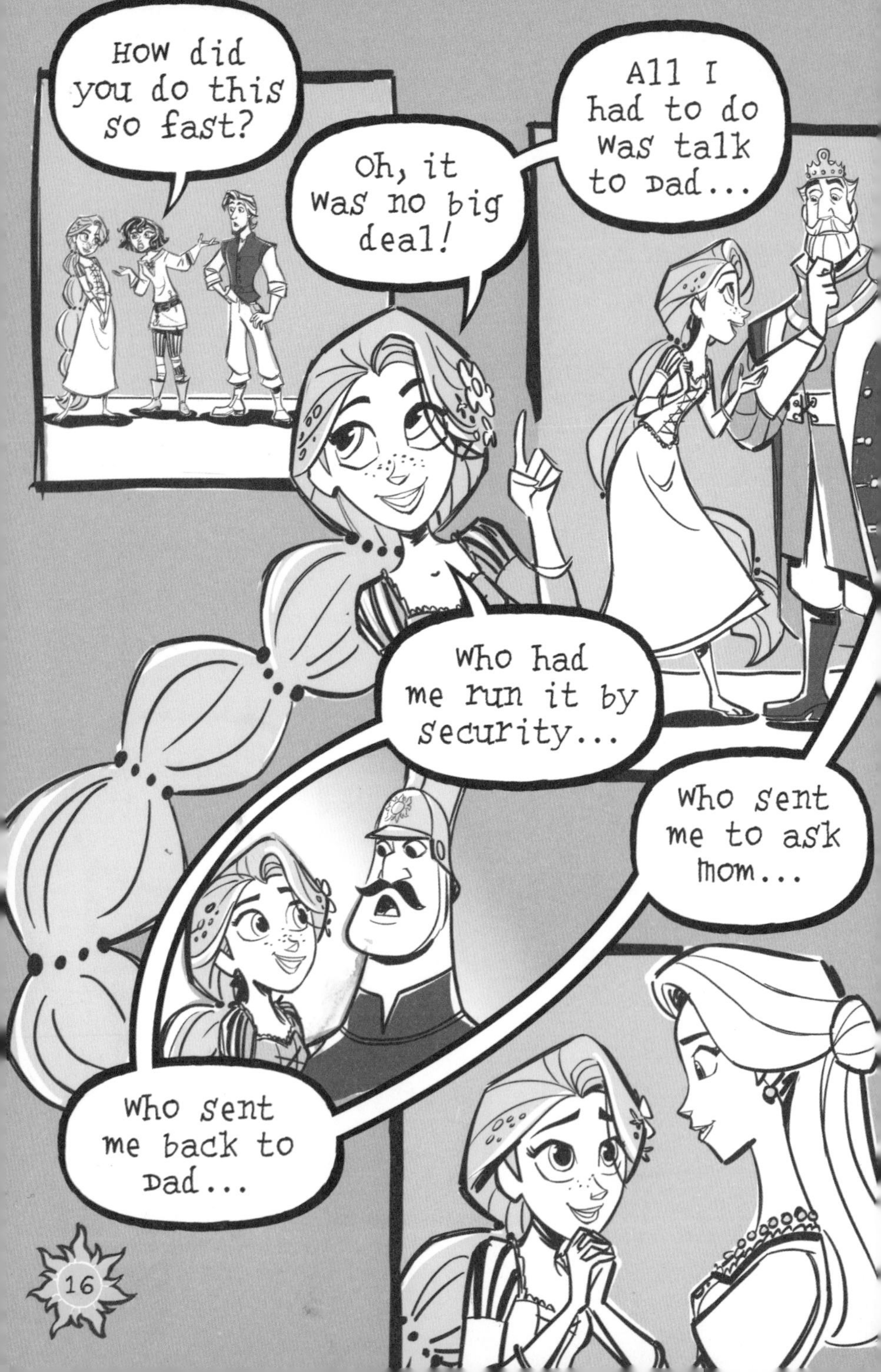
HOW did you do this so fast?
Oh, it was no big deal!
All I had to do was talk to Dad...
Who had me run it by security...
Who sent me to ask mom...
Who sent me back to Dad...

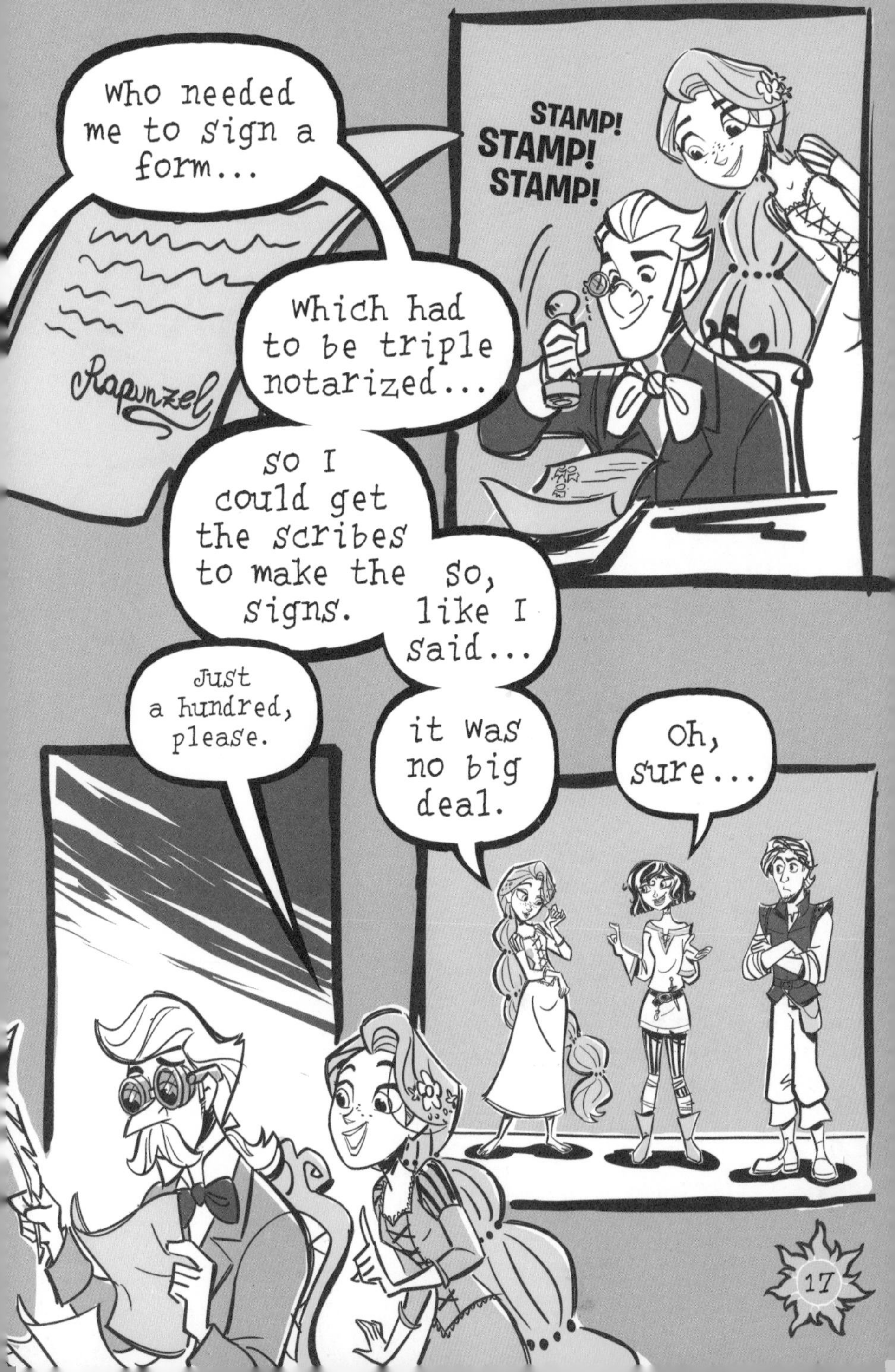
Who needed me to sign a form...
Rapunzel
STAMP!
STAMP!
STAMP!
Which had to be triple notarized...
So I could get the scribes to make the signs.
So, like I said...
Just a hundred, please.
it was no big deal.
Oh, sure...

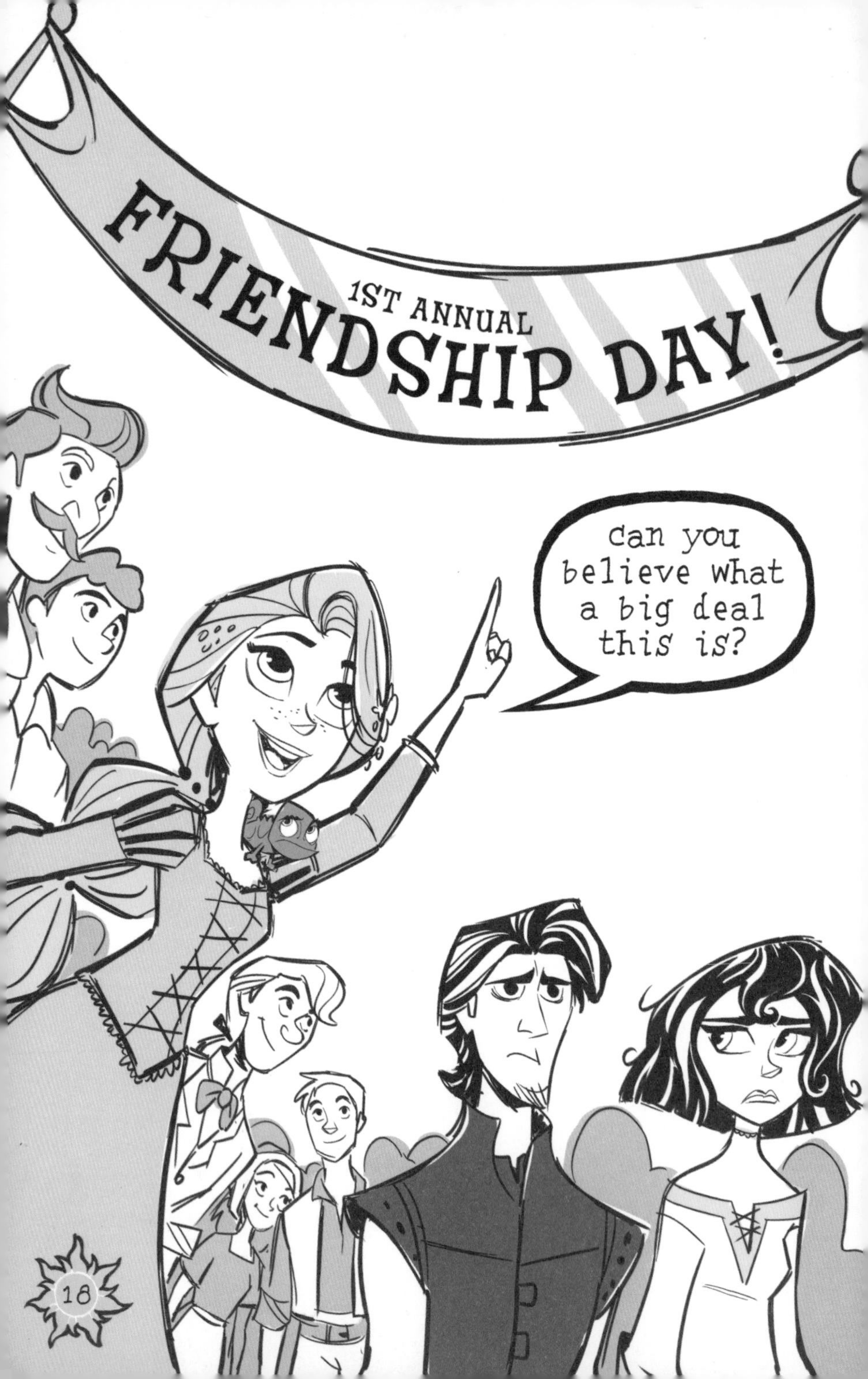
1ST ANNUAL
FRIENDSHIP DAY!
Can you believe what a big deal this is?

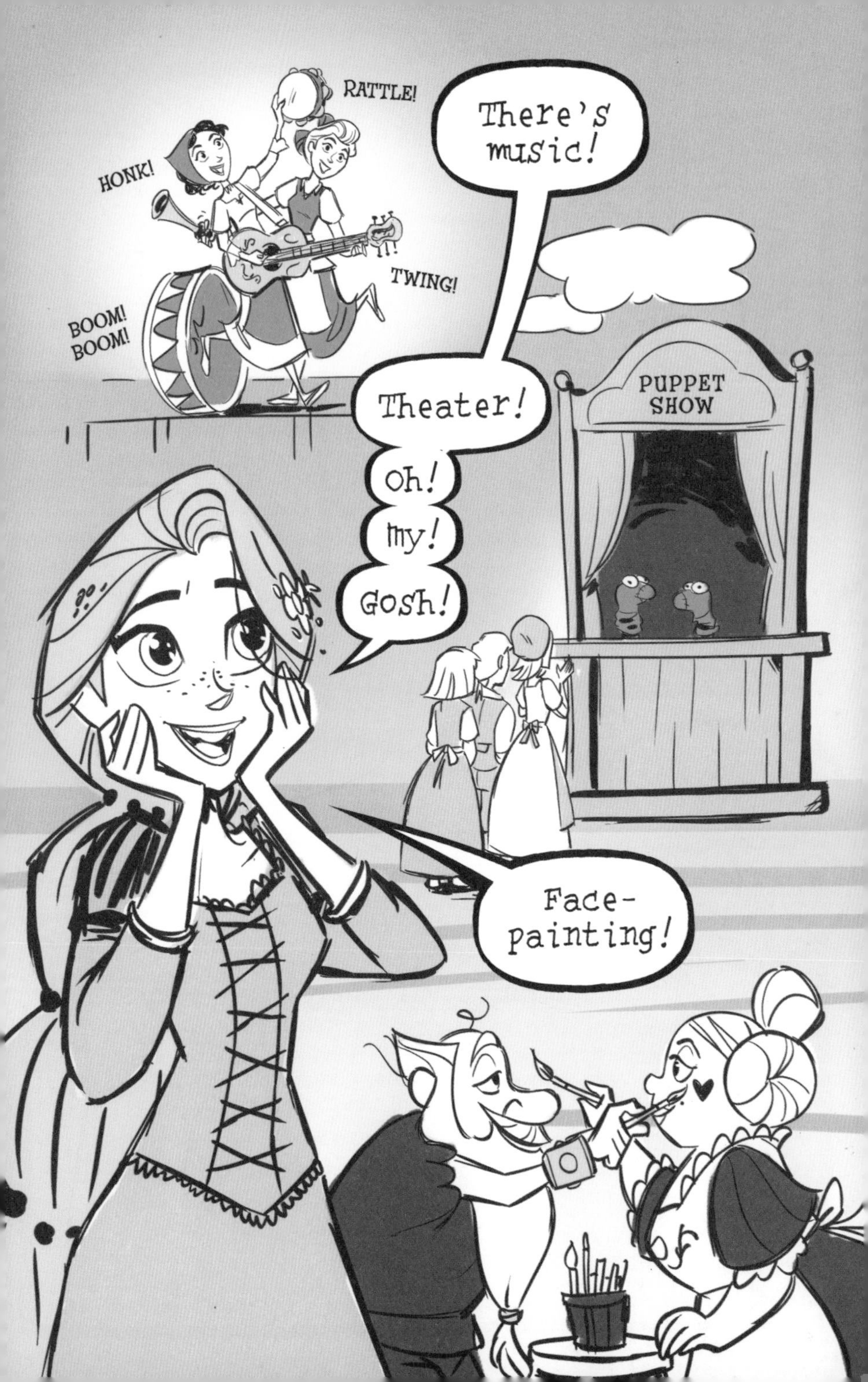
RATTLE!
HONK!
There's music!
TWING!
BOOM! BOOM!
Theater!
PUPPET SHOW
Oh!
my!
Gosh!
Face-painting!

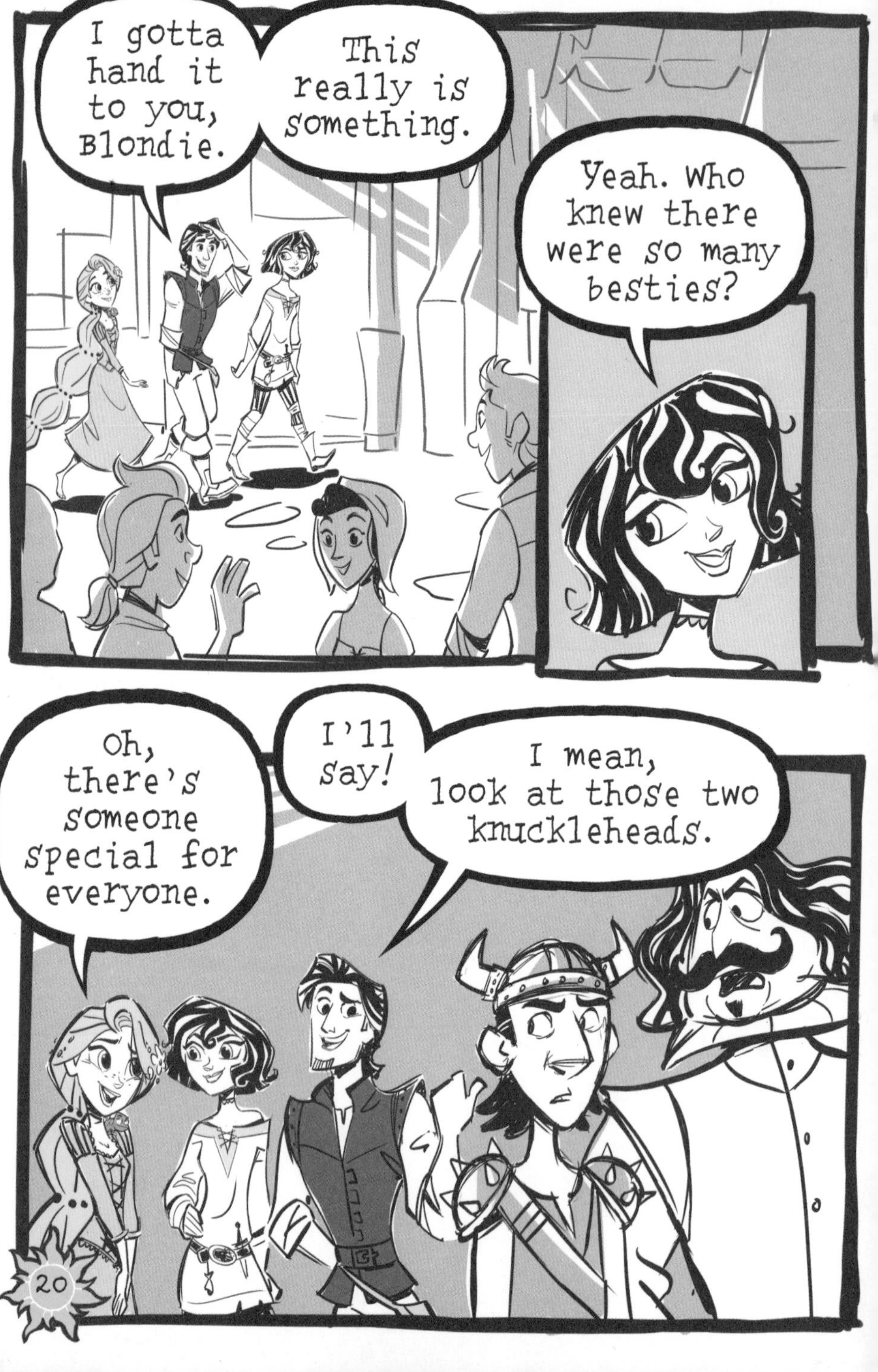
I gotta hand it to you, Blondie.
This really is something.
Yeah. Who knew there were so many besties?
Oh, there's someone special for everyone.
I'll say!
I mean, look at those two knuckleheads.

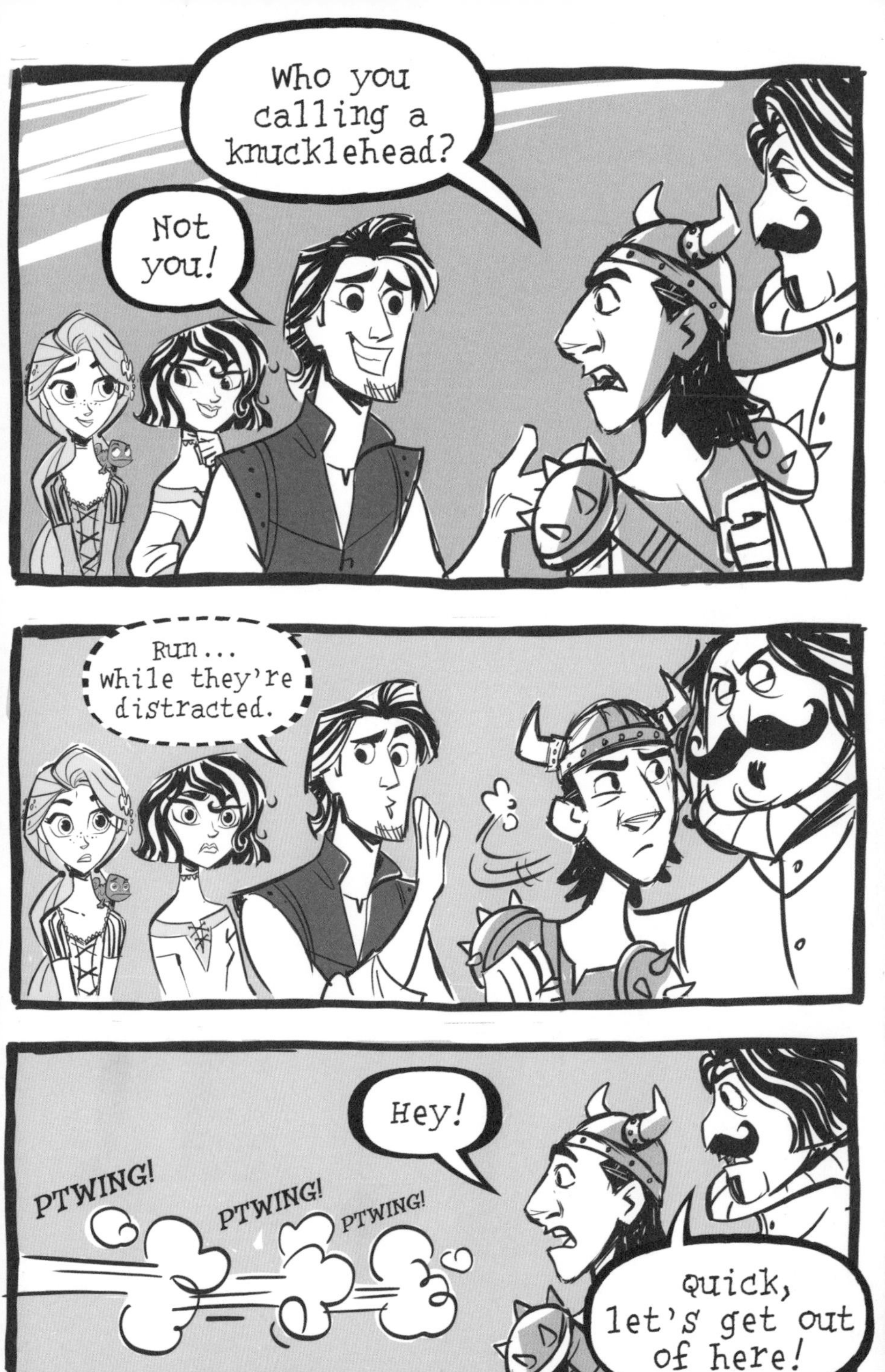
Who you calling a knucklehead?
Not you!
Run... while they're distracted.
Hey!
PTWING!
PTWING!
PTWING!
Quick, let's get out of here!

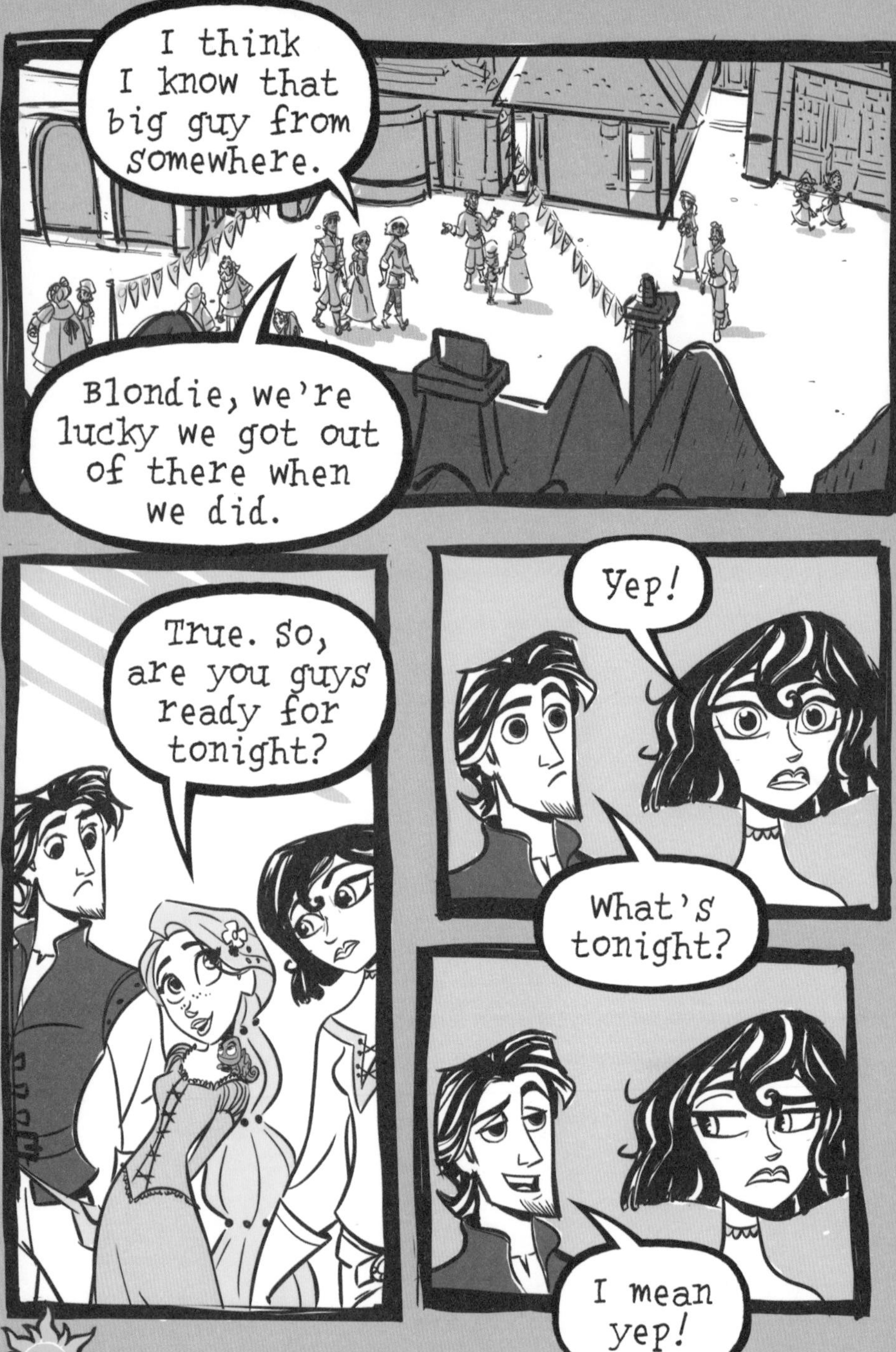
I think I know that big guy from somewhere.
Blondie, we're lucky we got out of there when we did.
True. So, are you guys ready for tonight?
Yep!
What's tonight?
I mean yep!

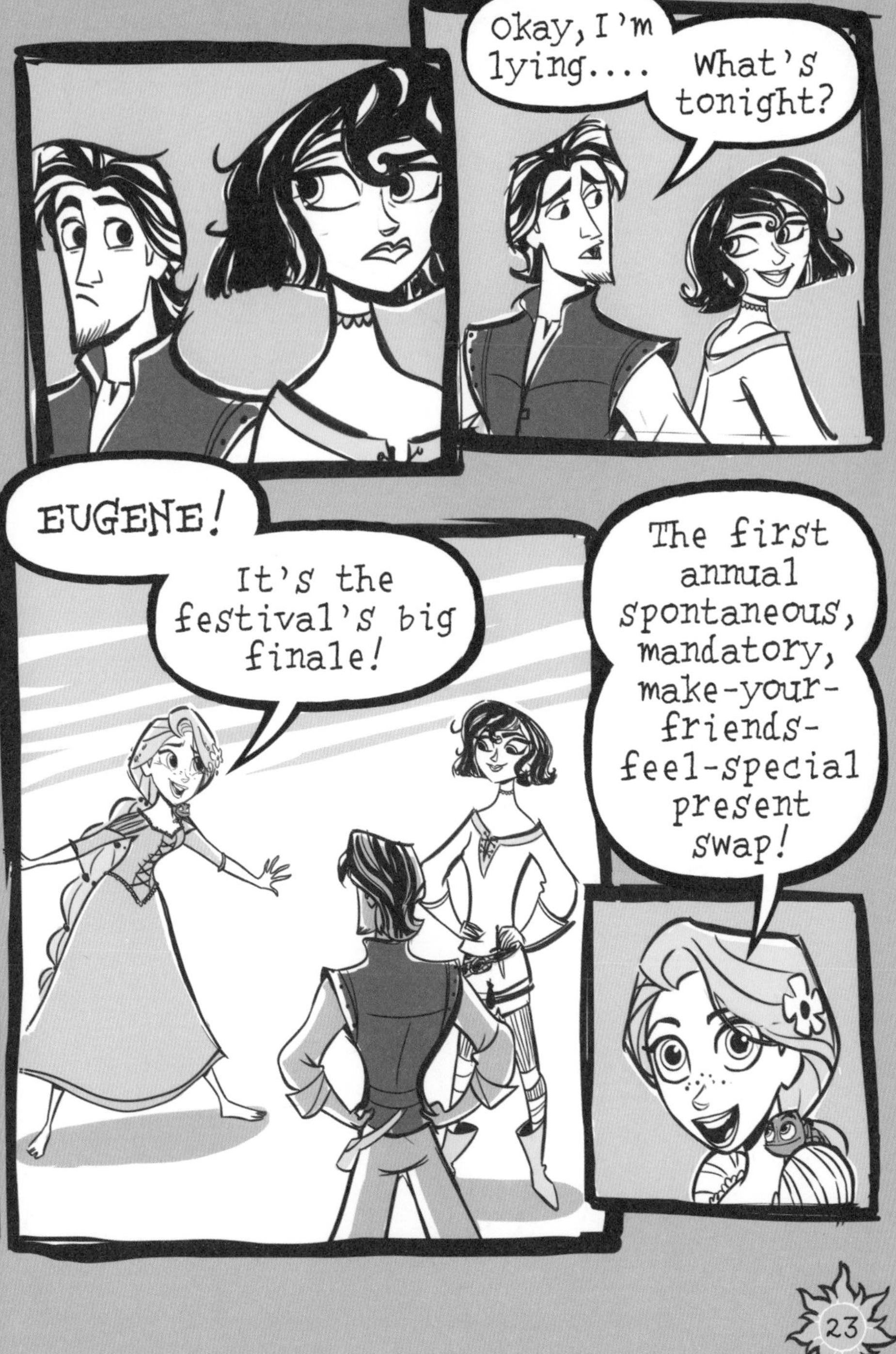
Okay, I'm lying....
What's tonight?
EUGENE!
It's the festival's big finale!
The first annual spontaneous, mandatory, make-your-friends-feel-special present swap!

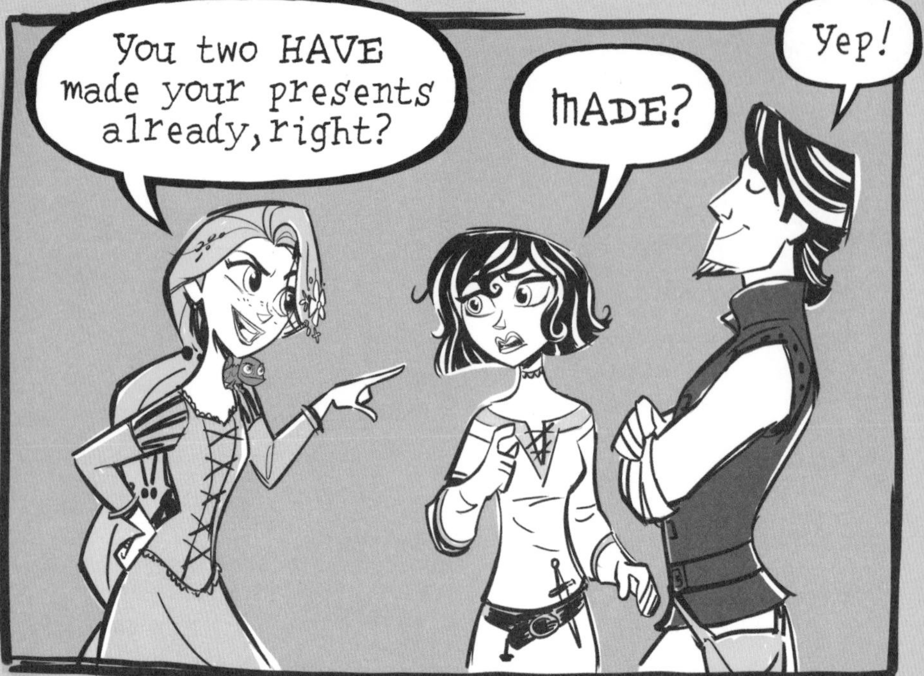
You two HAVE made your presents already, right?
MADE?
Yep!

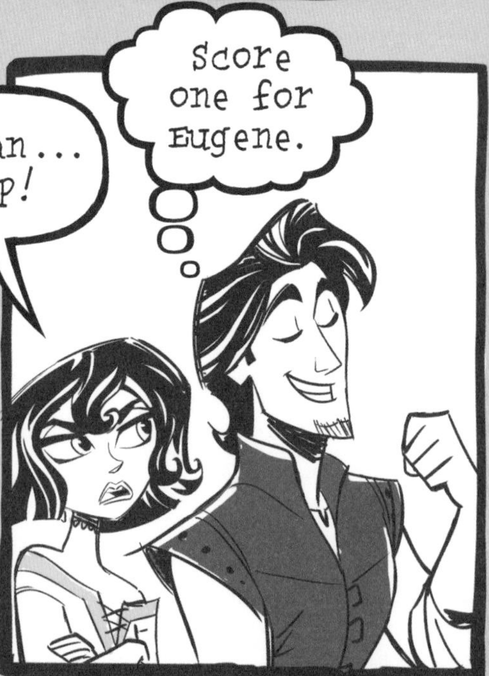
I mean... yep!
Score one for Eugene.

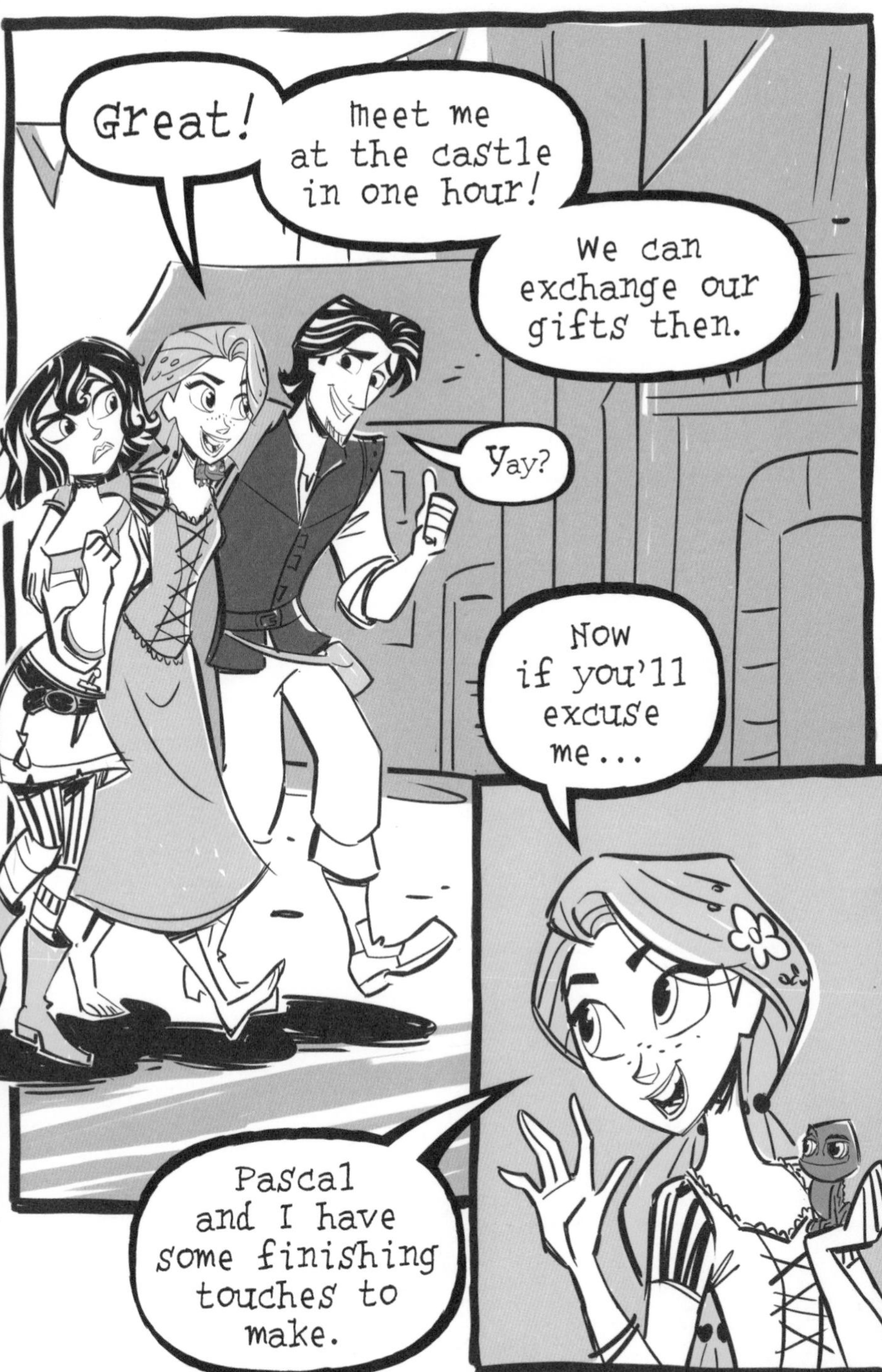
Great!
Meet me at the castle in one hour!
We can exchange our gifts then.
Yay?
Now if you'll excuse me...
Pascal and I have some finishing touches to make.

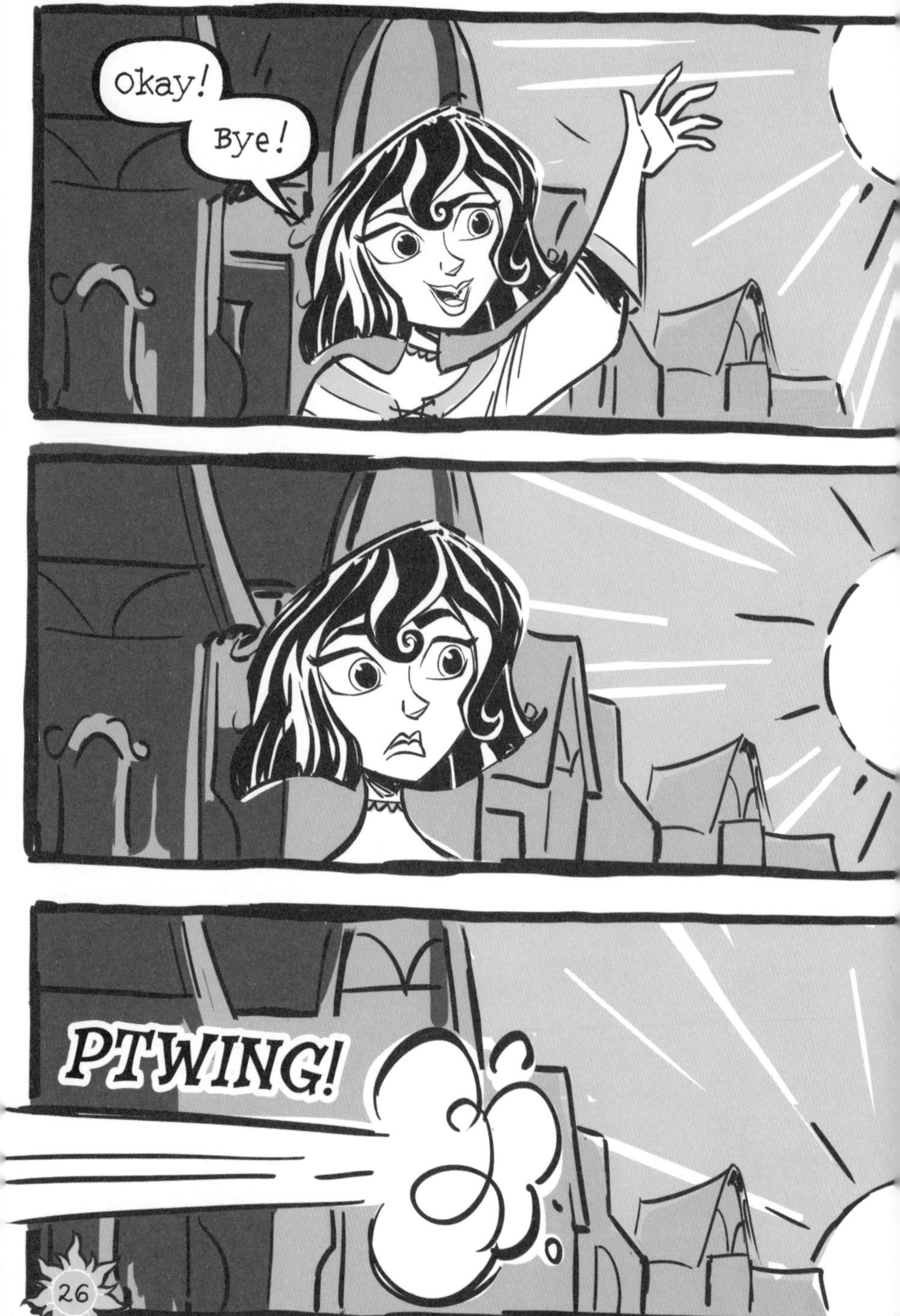
Okay!
Bye!
PTWING!

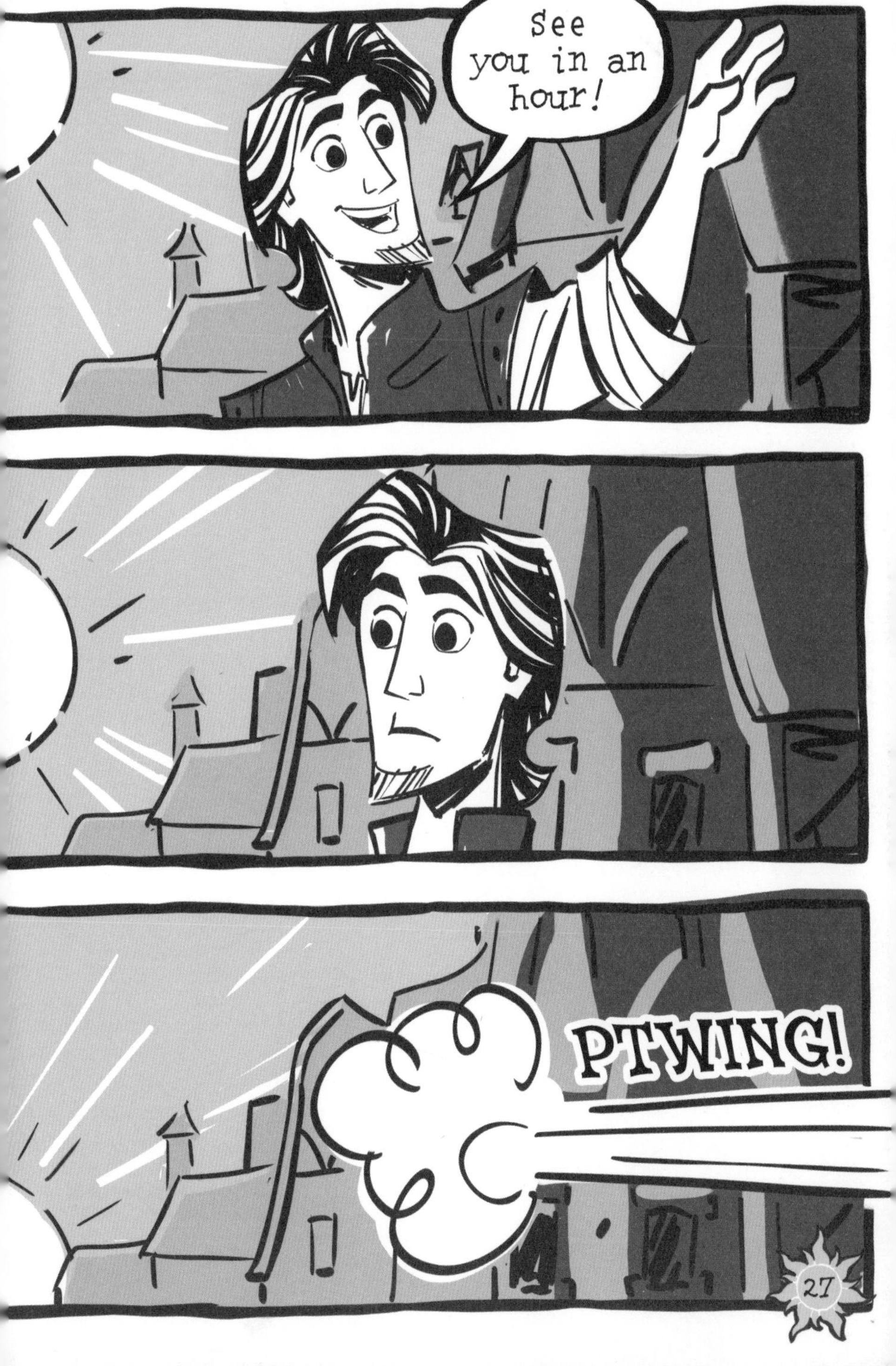
See you in an hour!
PTWING!

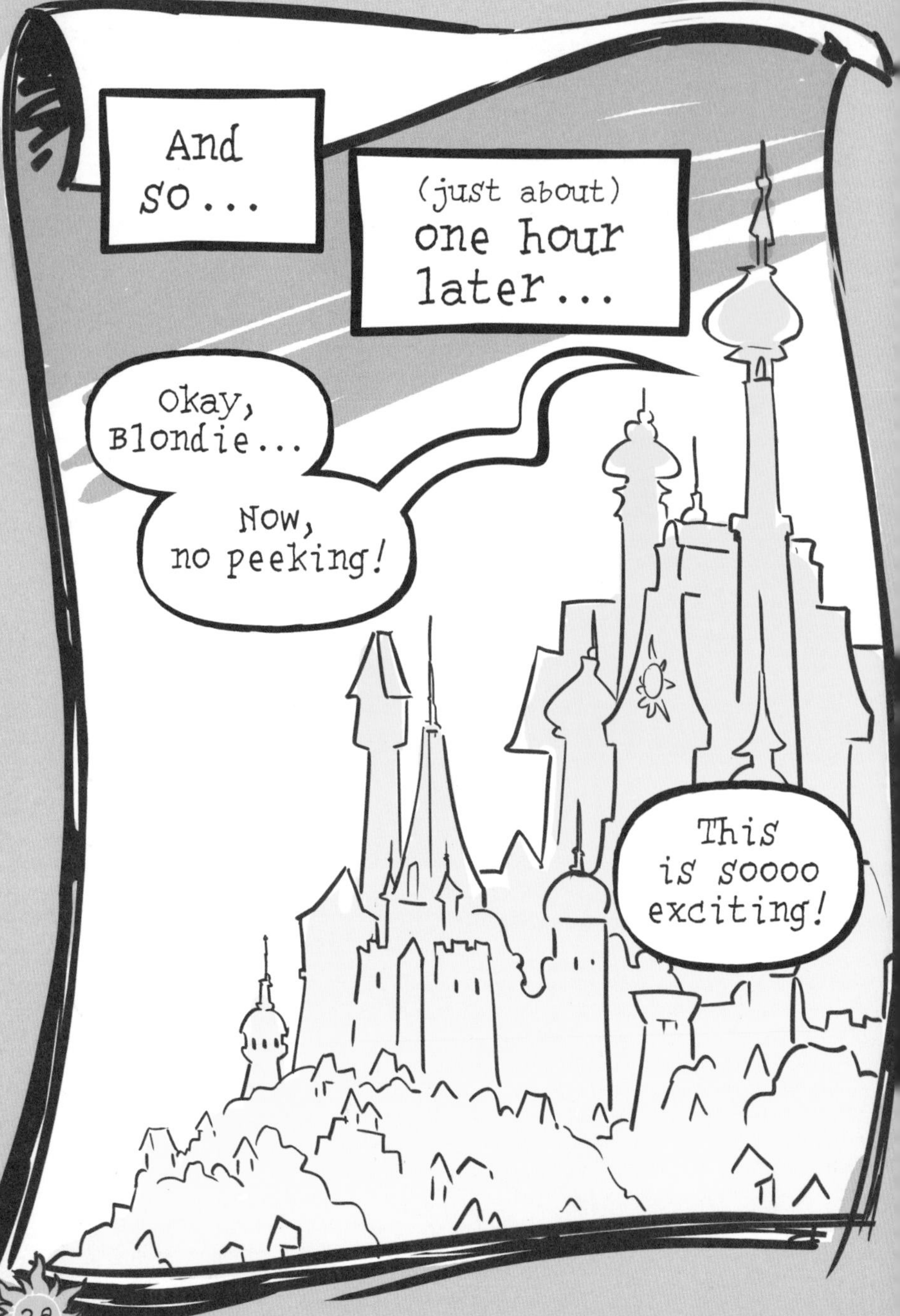
And so...
(just about) one hour later...
Okay, Blondie...
Now, no peeking!
This is soooo exciting!

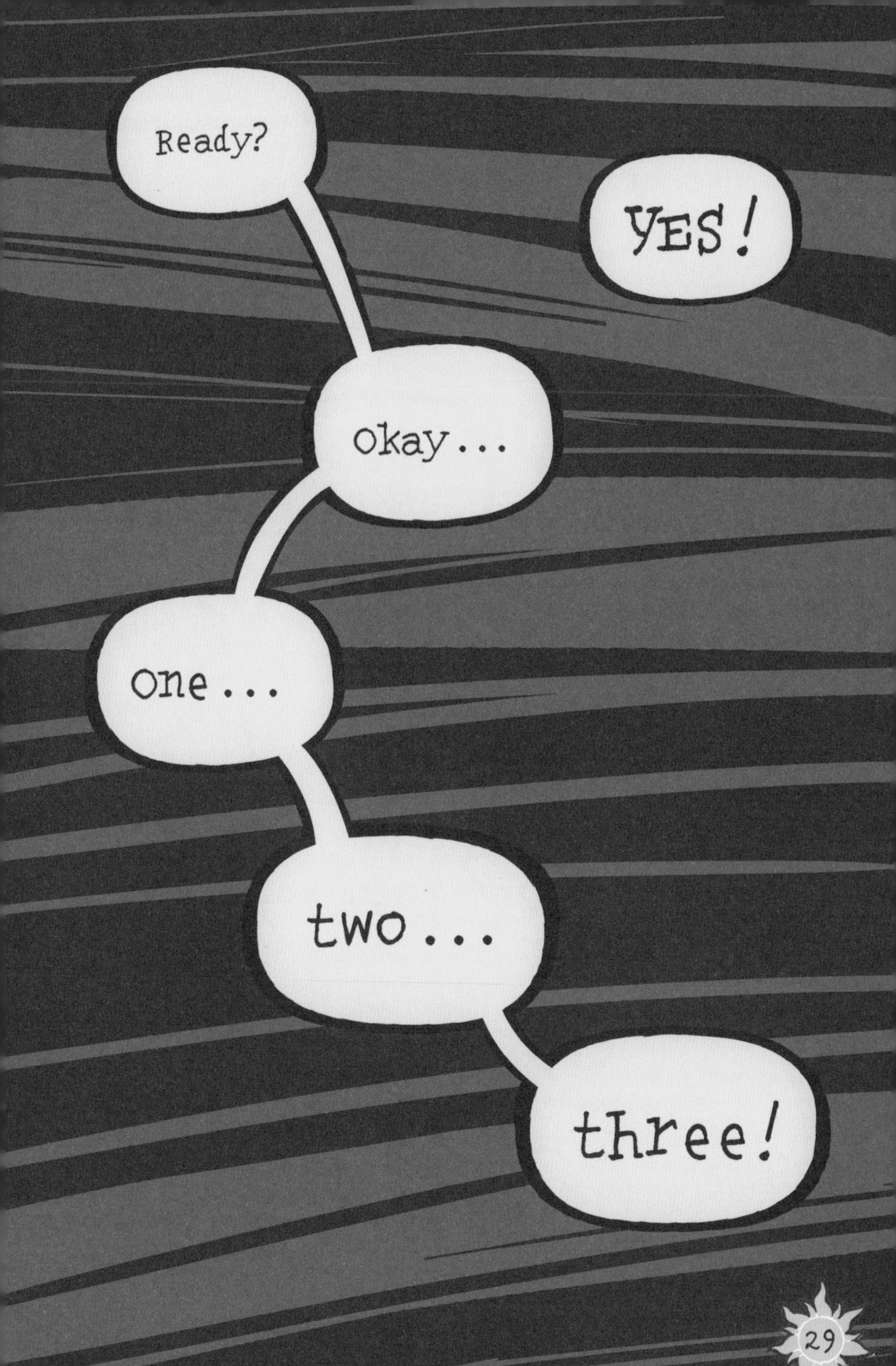
Ready?
YES!
Okay...
One...
two...
three!

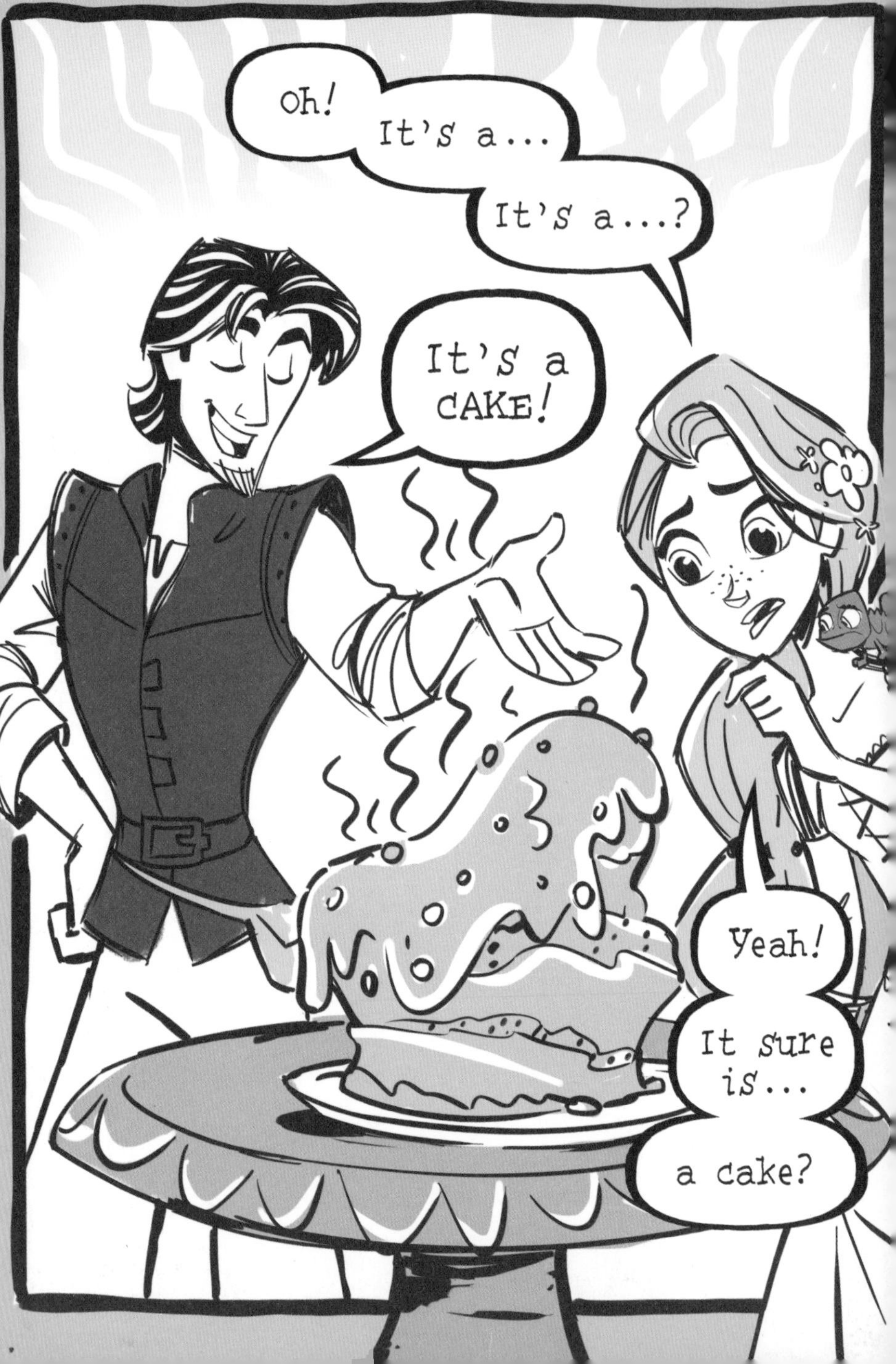
Oh!
It's a...
It's a...?
It's a CAKE!
Yeah!
It sure is...
a cake?

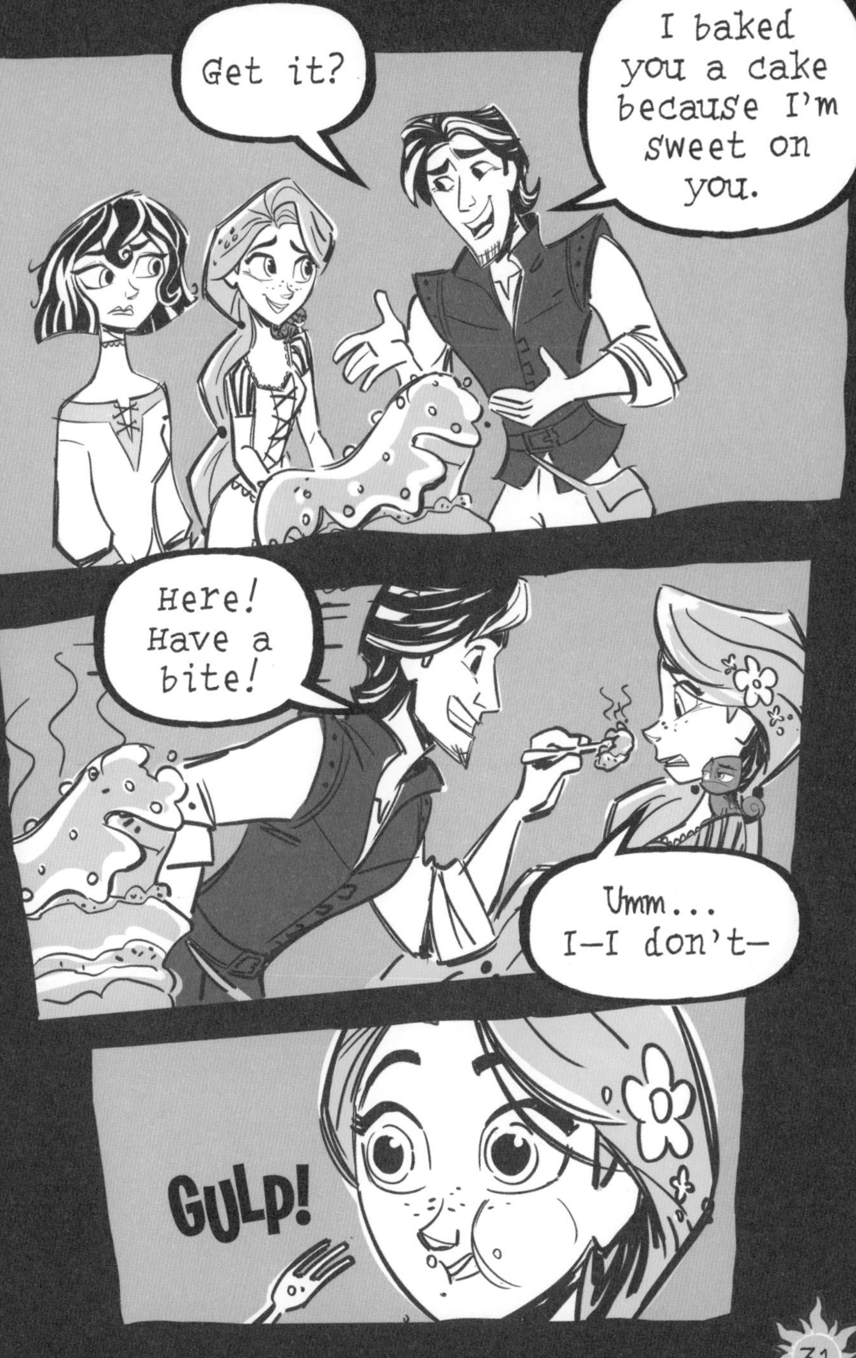
Get it?
I baked you a cake because I'm sweet on you.
Here! Have a bite!
Umm... I—I don't—
GULP!

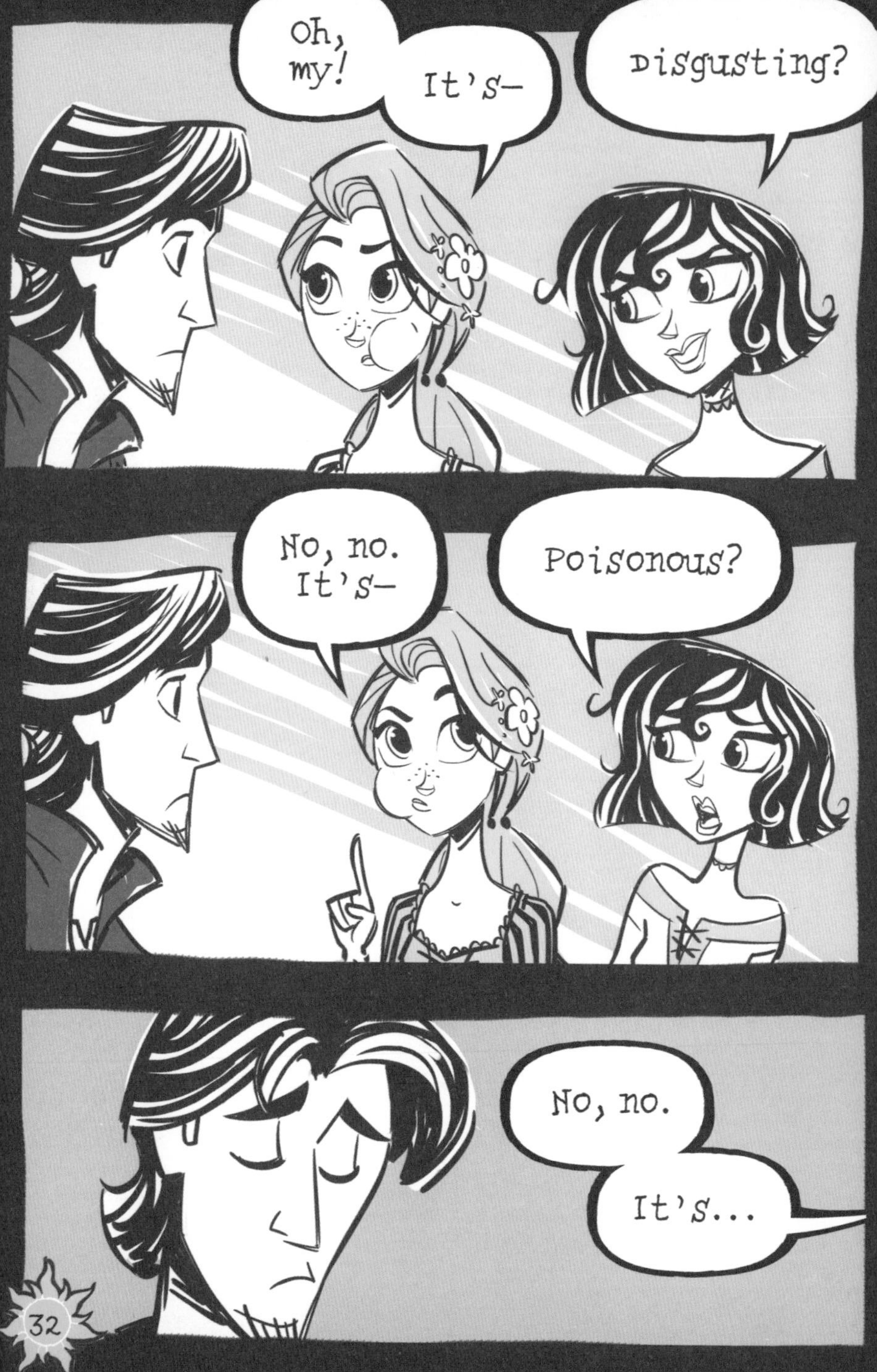
Oh, my!
It's–
Disgusting?
No, no. It's–
Poisonous?
No, no.
It's...

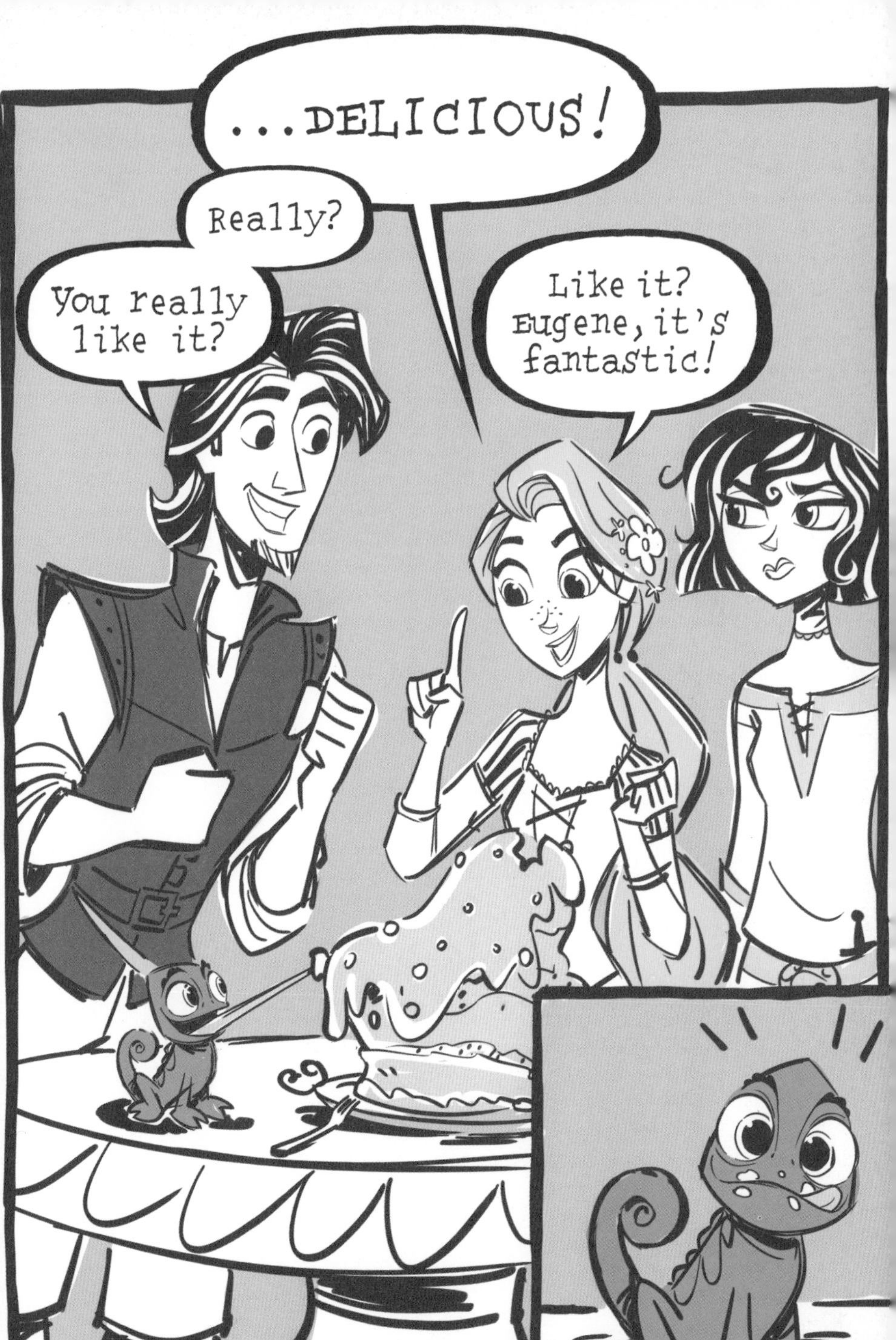
...DELICIOUS!
Really?
You really like it?
Like it? Eugene, it's fantastic!

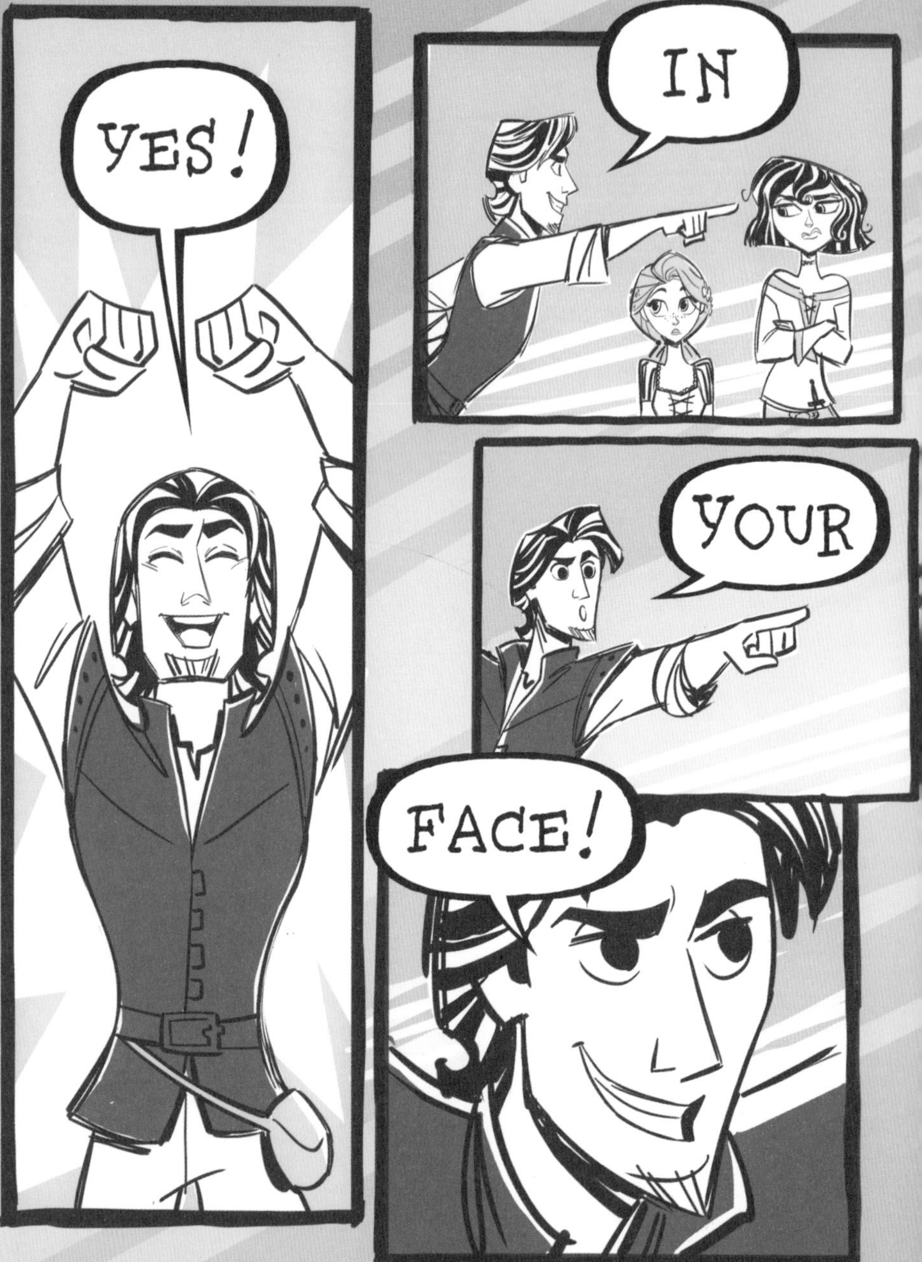
YES!
IN
YOUR
FACE!

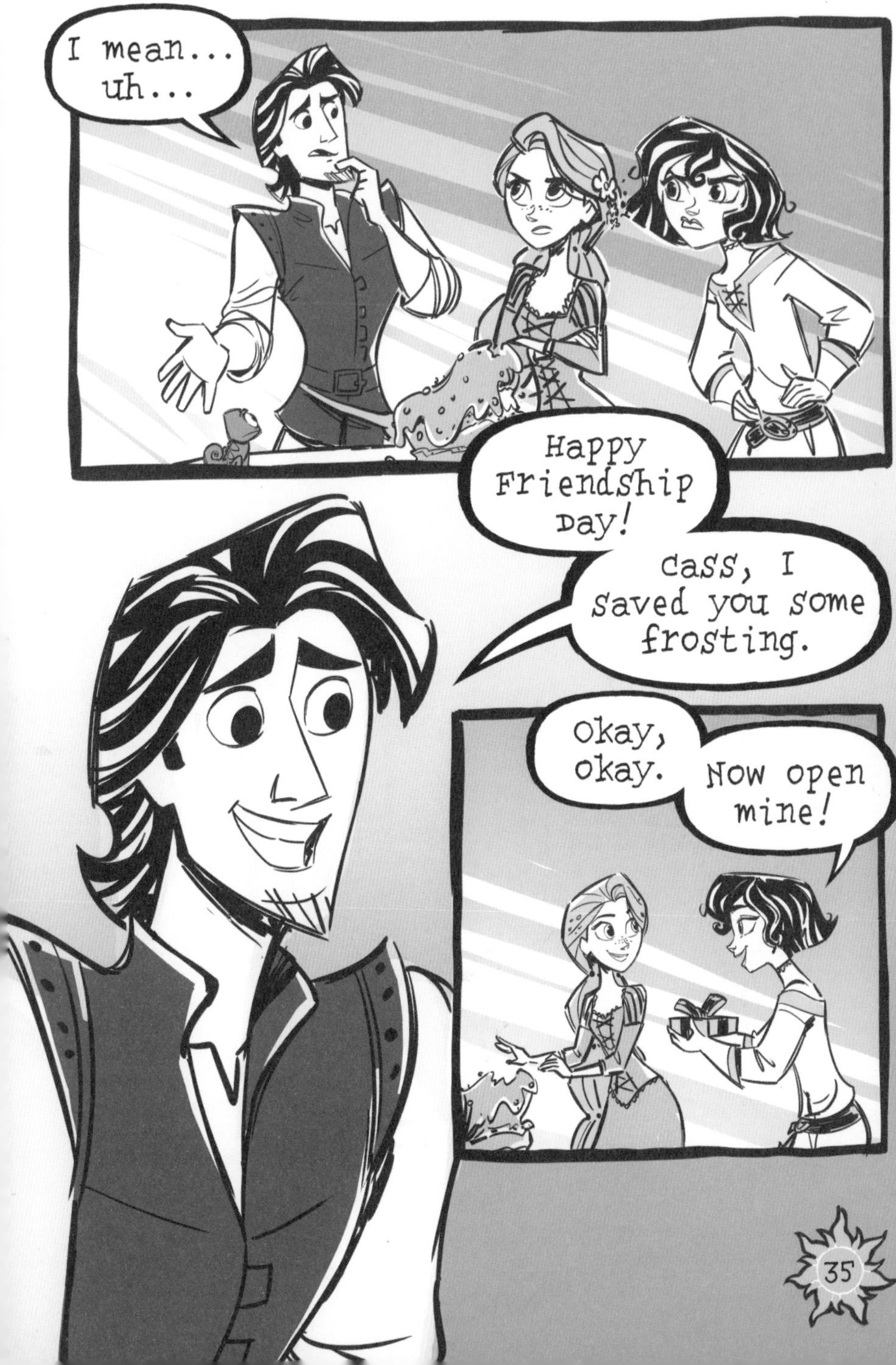

I mean...
uh...
Happy Friendship Day!
Cass, I saved you some frosting.
Okay, okay.
Now open mine!

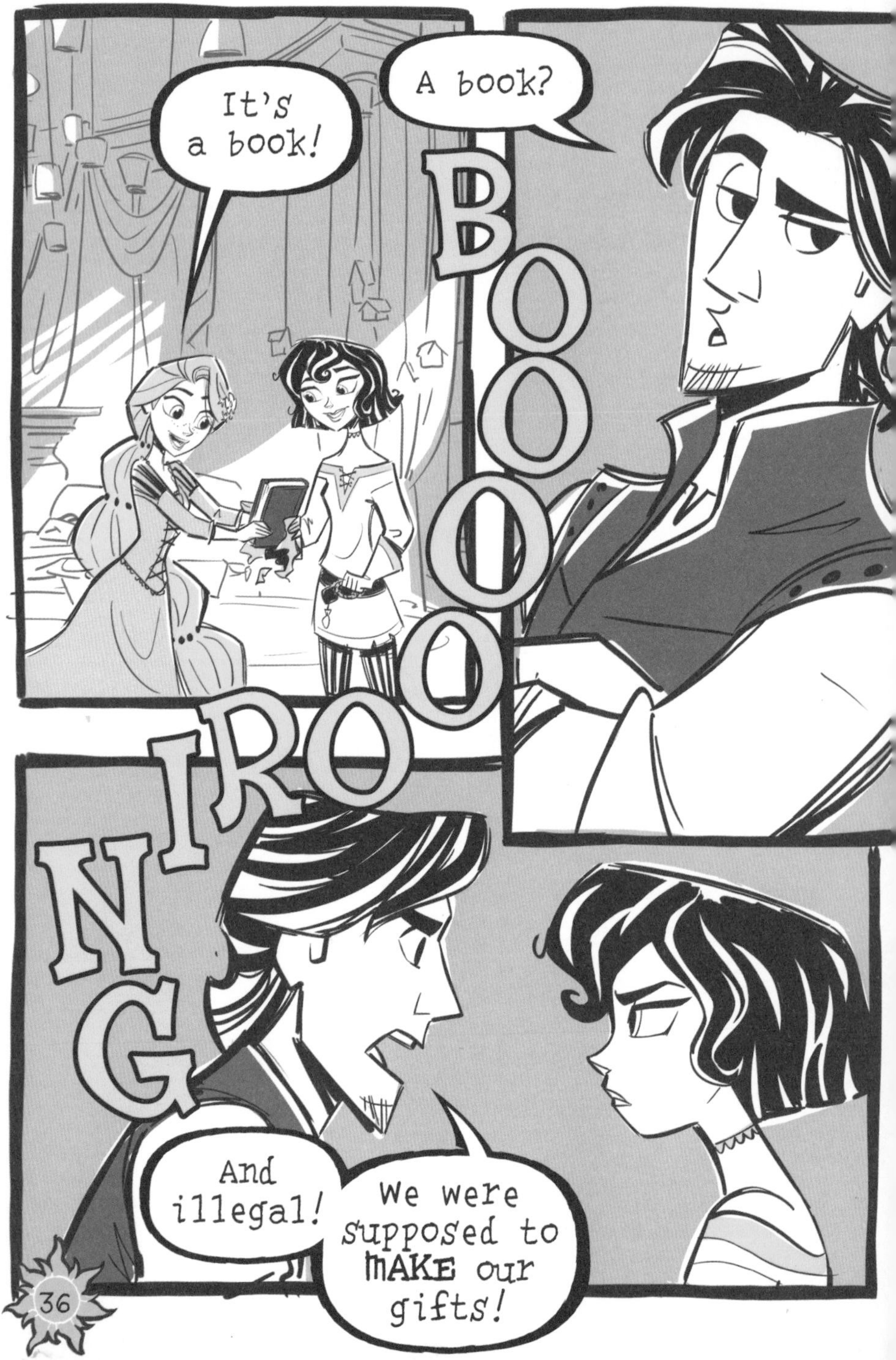

It's a book!
A book?
BOOOOOORING
And illegal!
We were supposed to MAKE our gifts!

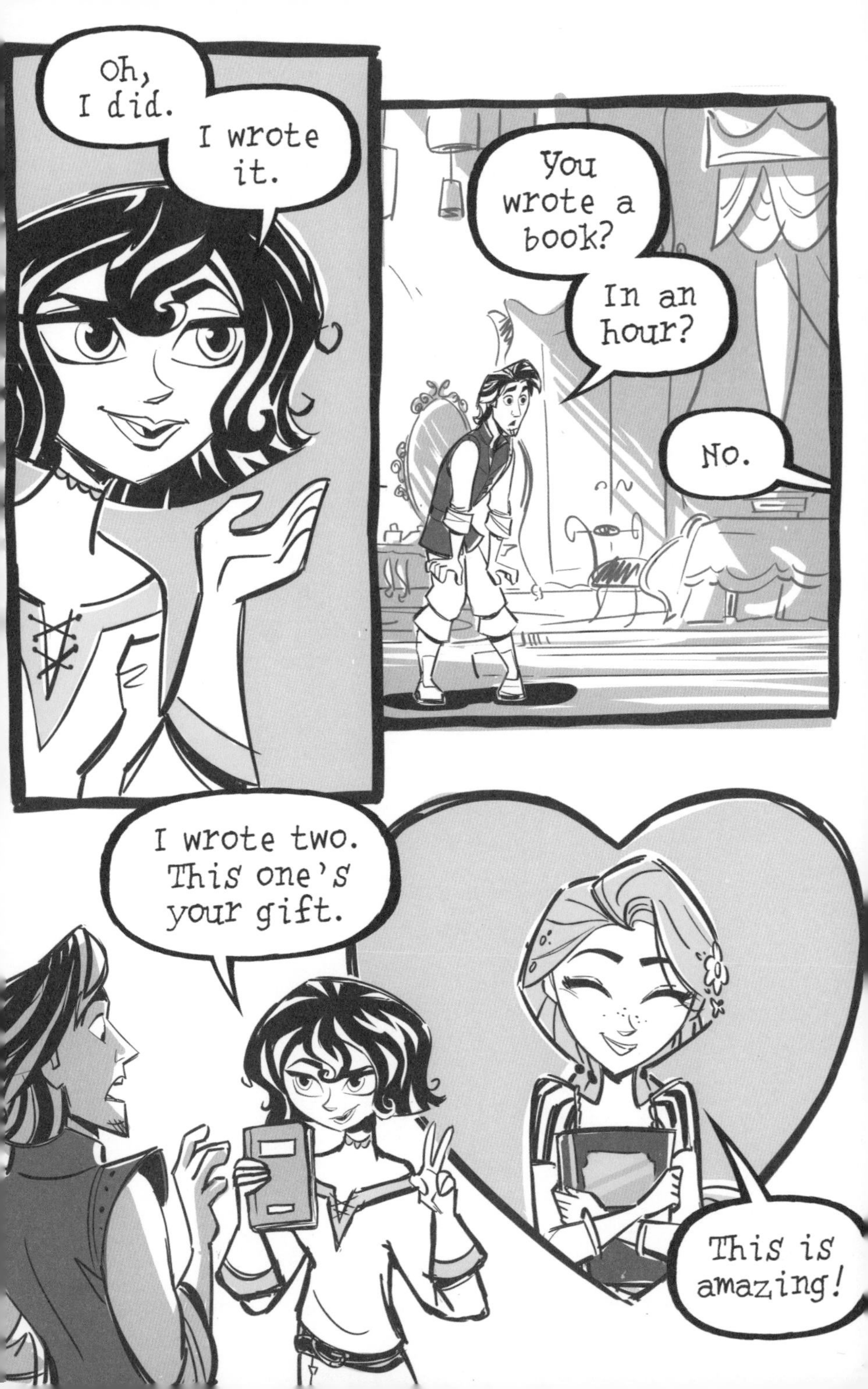
Oh, I did.
I wrote it.
You wrote a book?
In an hour?
No.
I wrote two. This one's your gift.
This is amazing!

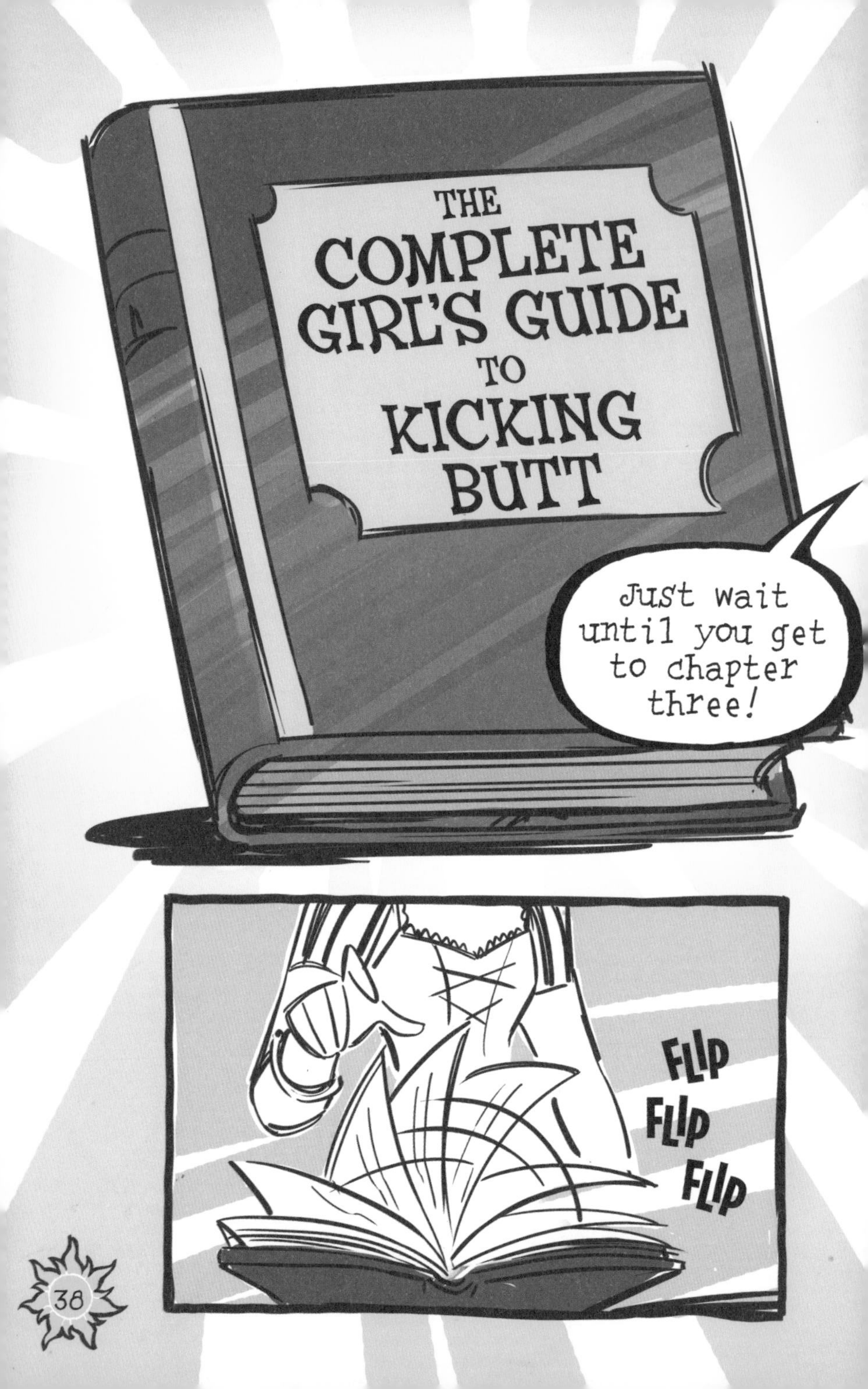
THE COMPLETE GIRL'S GUIDE TO KICKING BUTT
Just wait until you get to chapter three!
FLIP
FLIP
FLIP

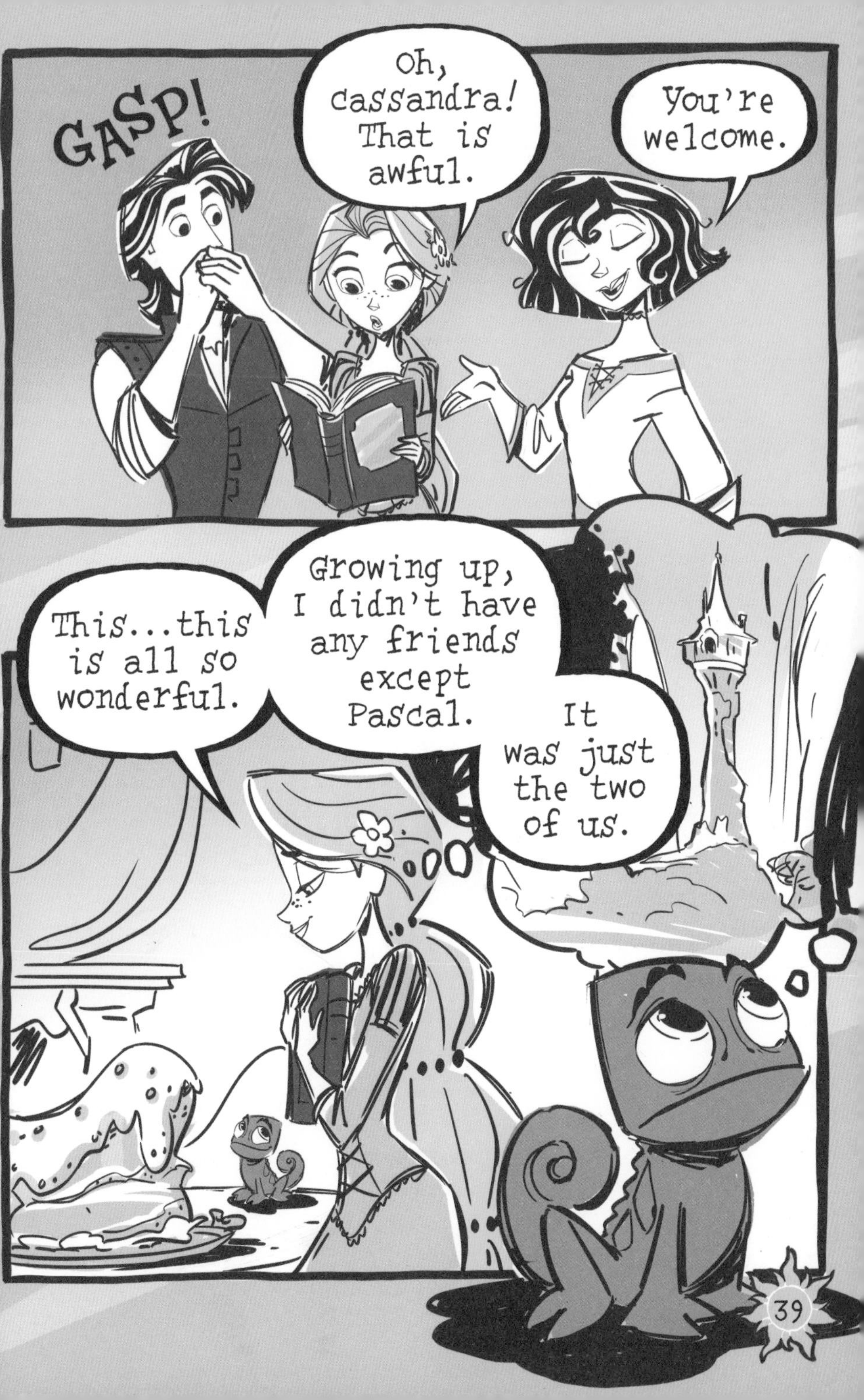
GASP!
Oh, cassandra! That is awful.
You're welcome.
This...this is all so wonderful.
Growing up, I didn't have any friends except Pascal.
It was just the two of us.

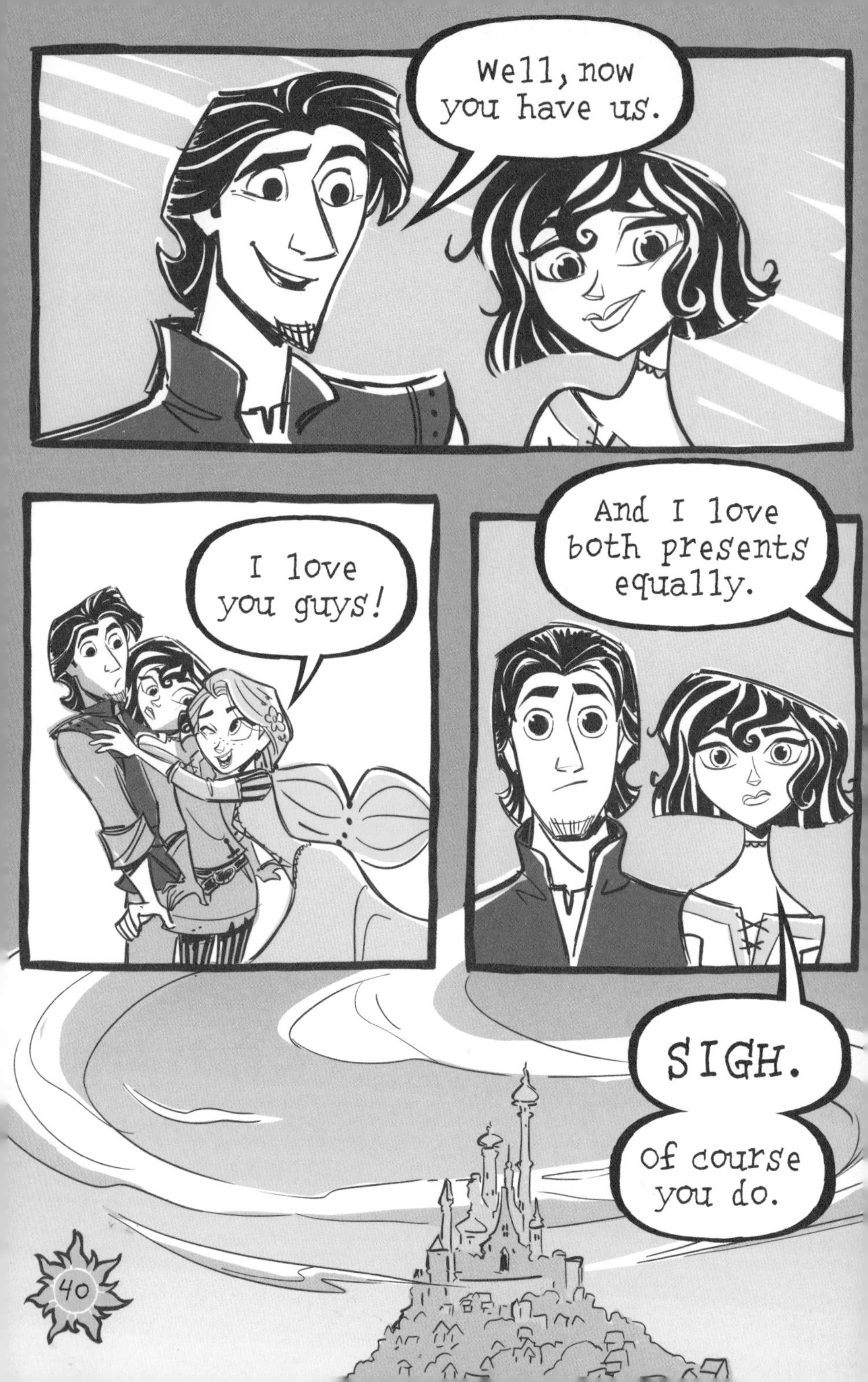
Well, now you have us.
I love you guys!
And I love both presents equally.
SIGH.
Of course you do.

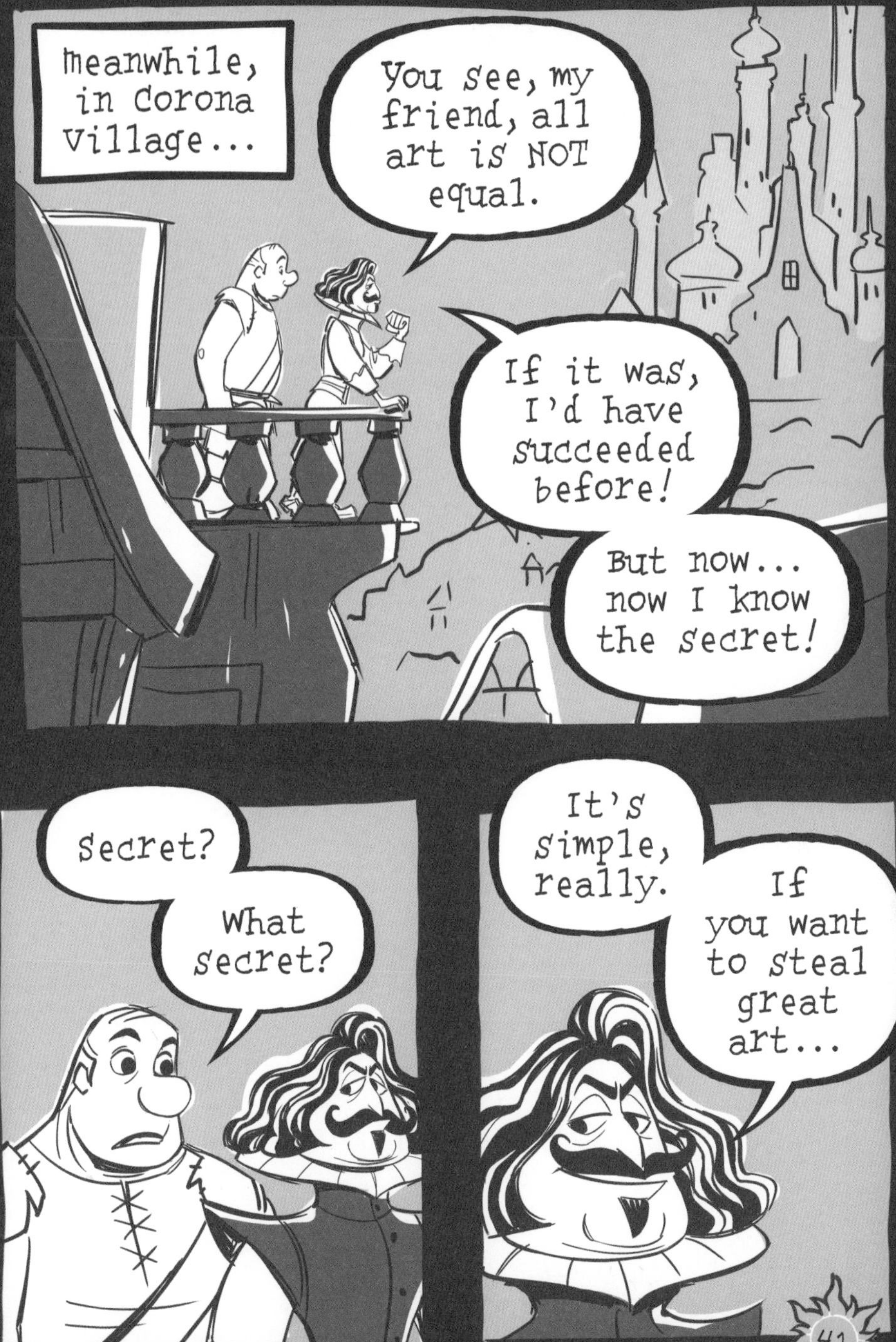
Meanwhile, in Corona Village...
You see, my friend, all art is NOT equal.
If it was, I'd have succeeded before!
But now... now I know the secret!
Secret?
What secret?
It's simple, really.
If you want to steal great art...

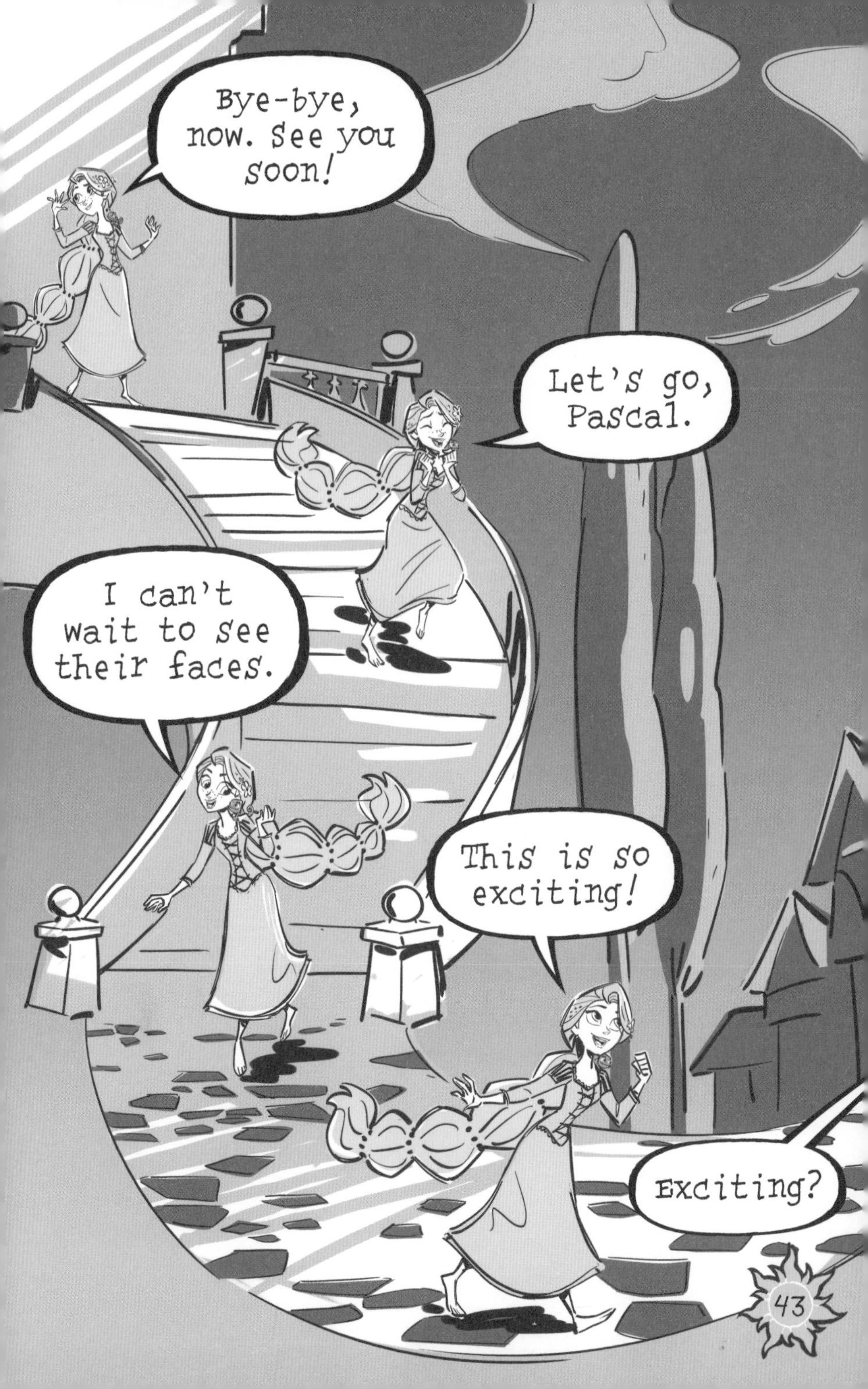
Bye-bye, now. See you soon!
Let's go, Pascal.
I can't wait to see their faces.
This is so exciting!
Exciting?

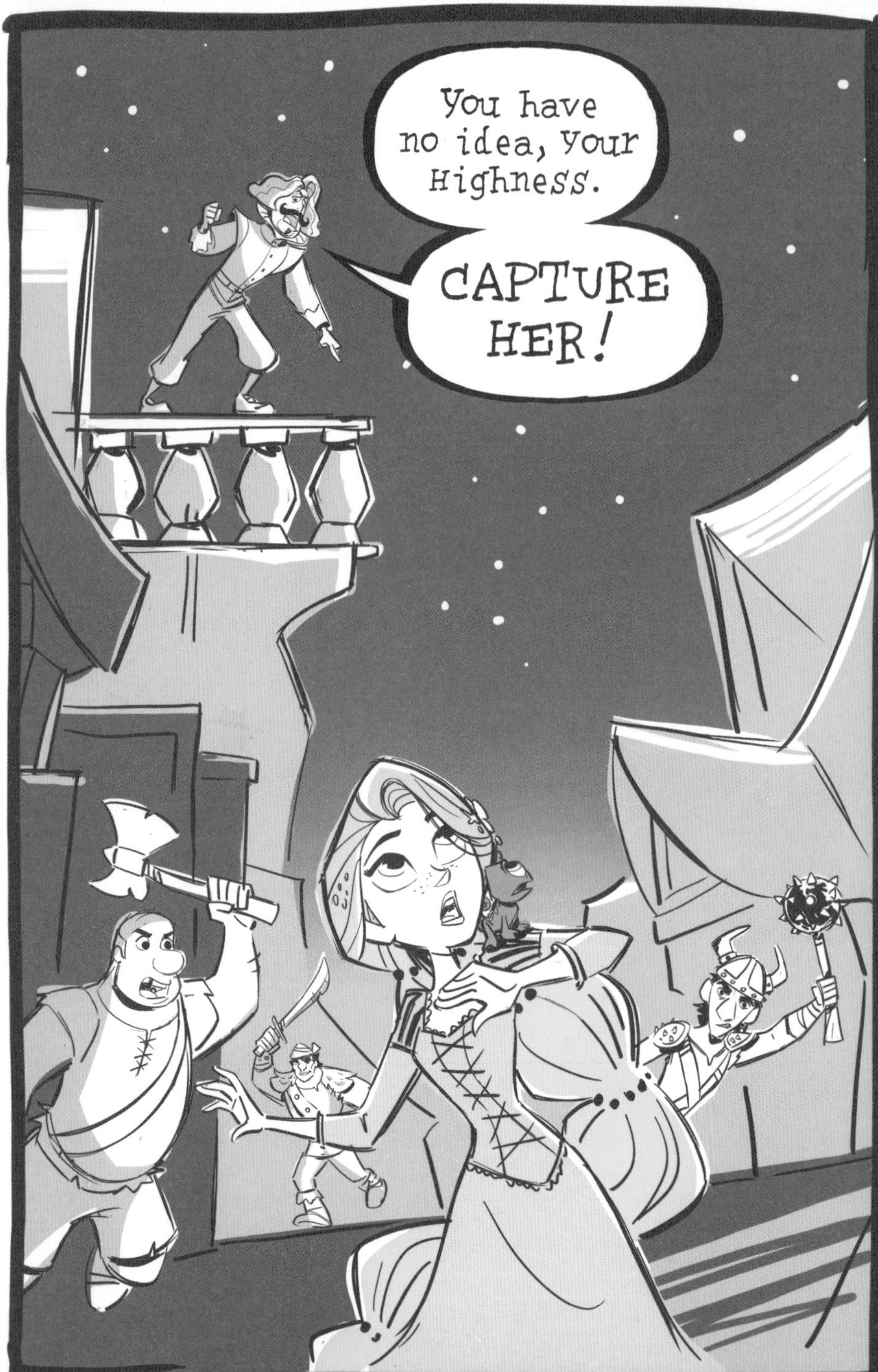
You have no idea, your Highness.
CAPTURE HER!

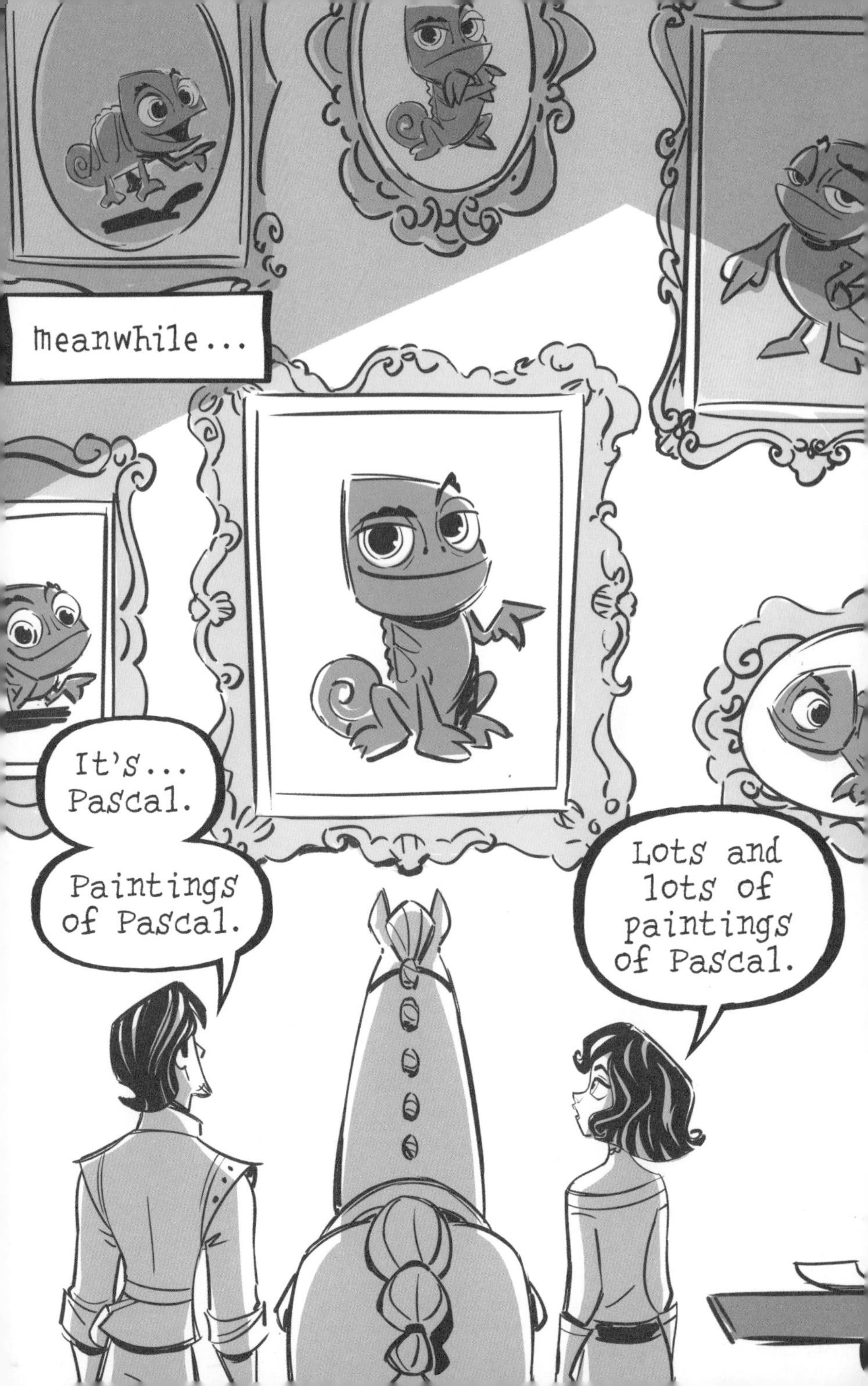
Meanwhile...
It's... Pascal.
Paintings of Pascal.
Lots and lots of paintings of Pascal.

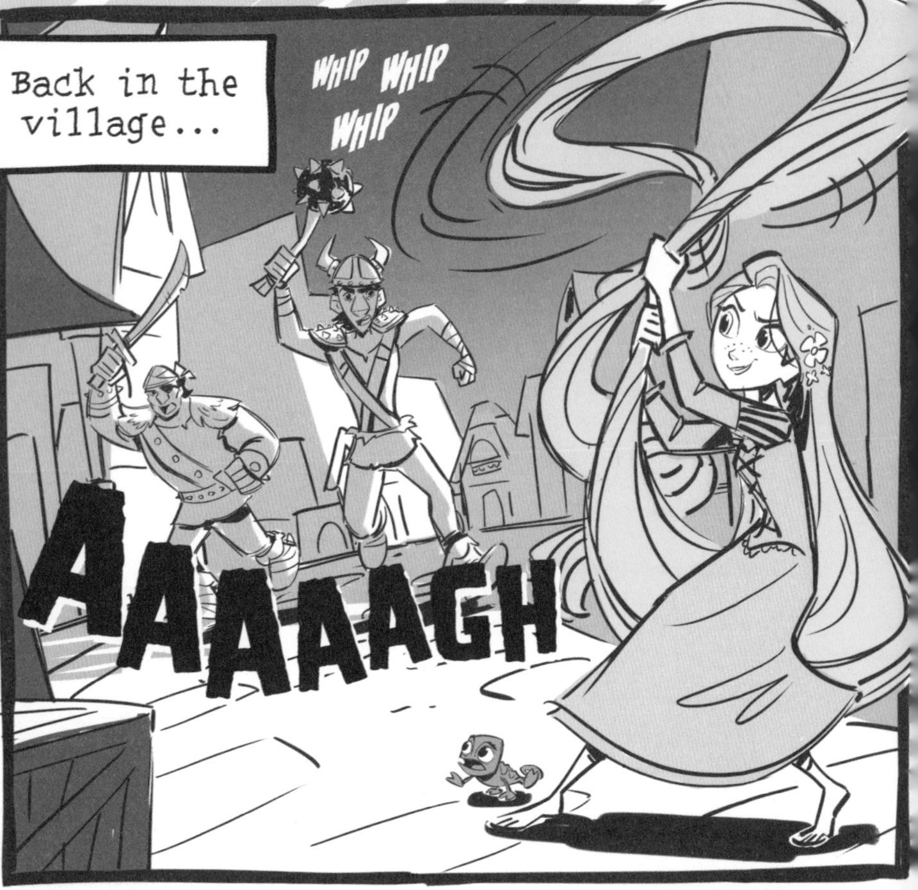
Back in the village...
WHIP WHIP
WHIP
AAAAAGH
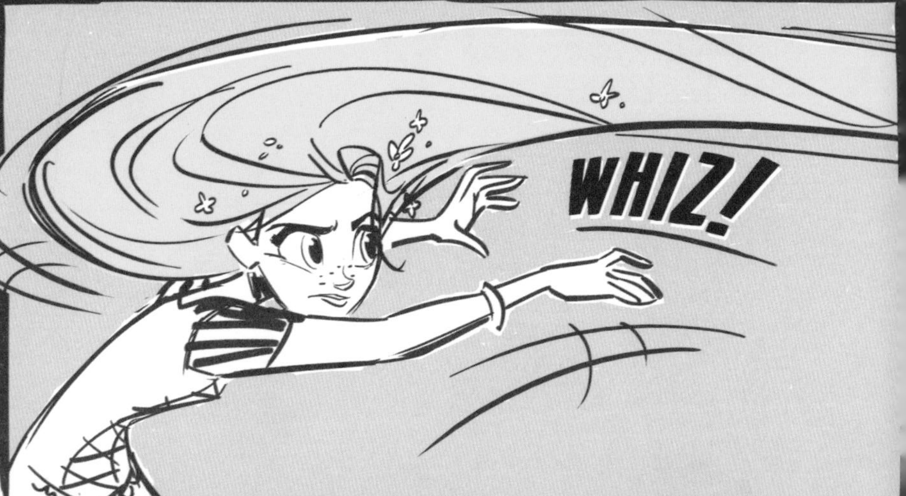
WHIZ!

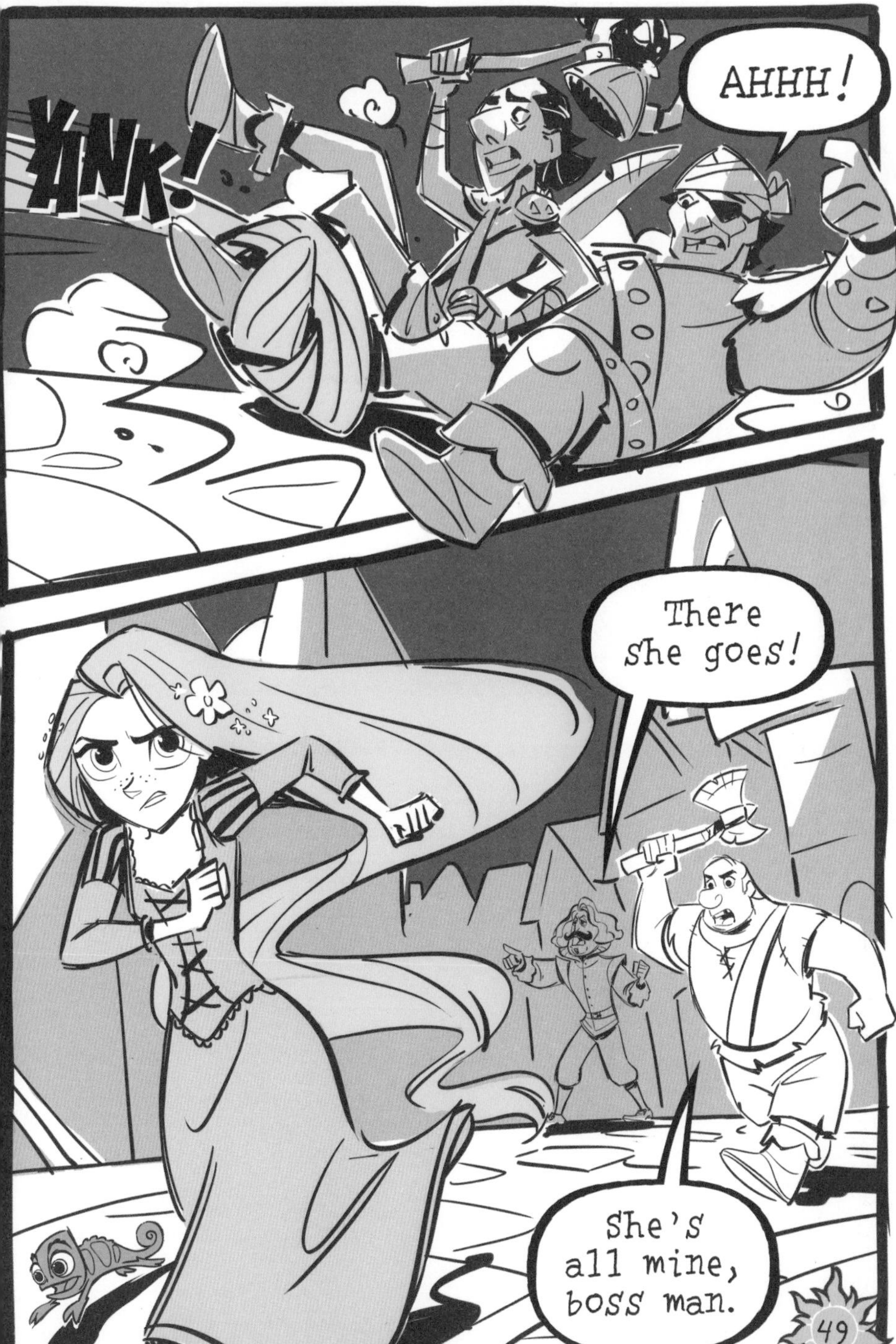
YANK!
AHHH!
There she goes!
She's all mine, boss man.

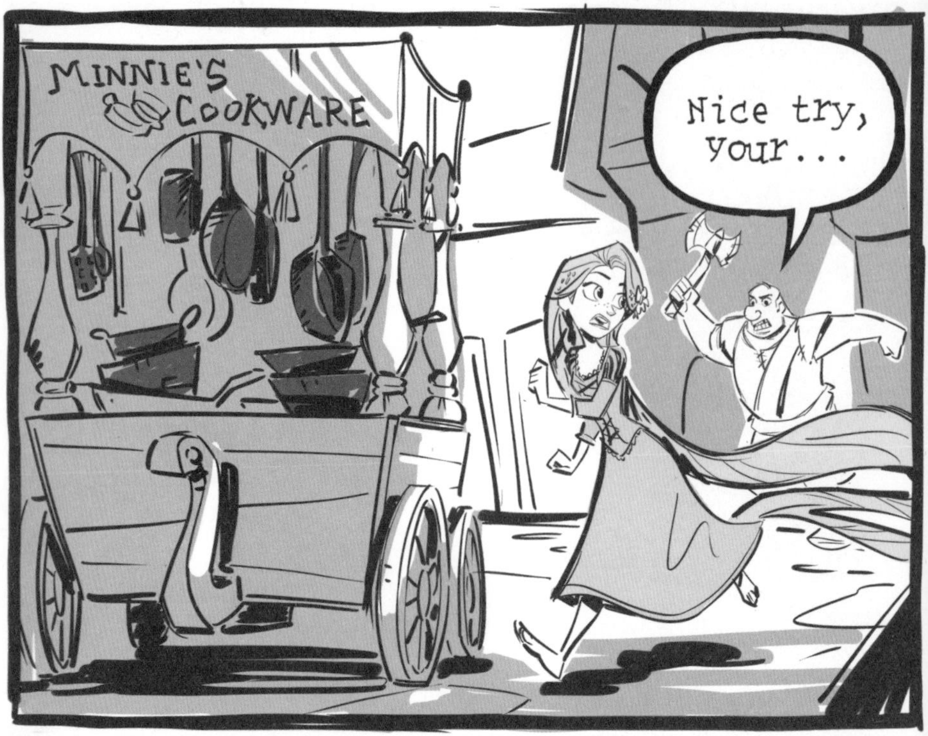
MINNIE'S COOKWARE
Nice try, your...

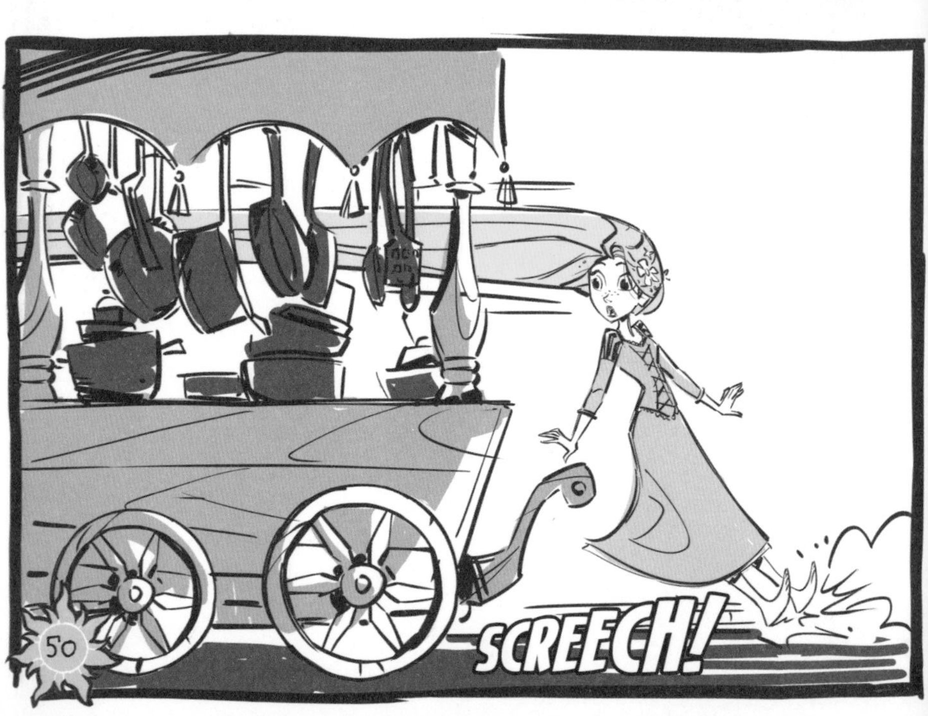
SCREECH!

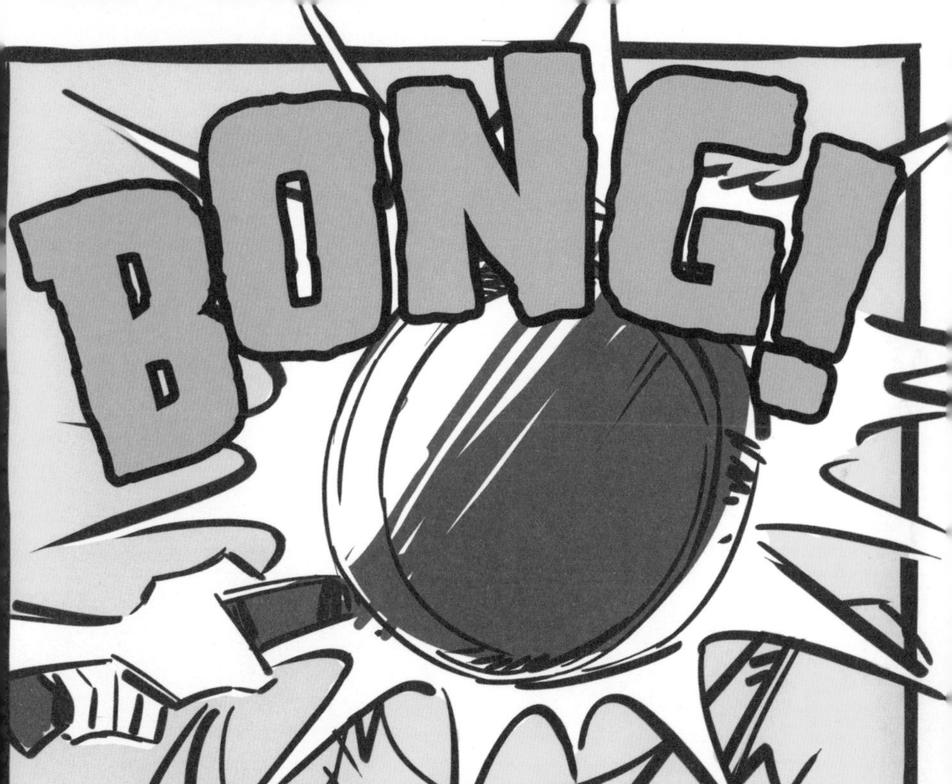
BONG!

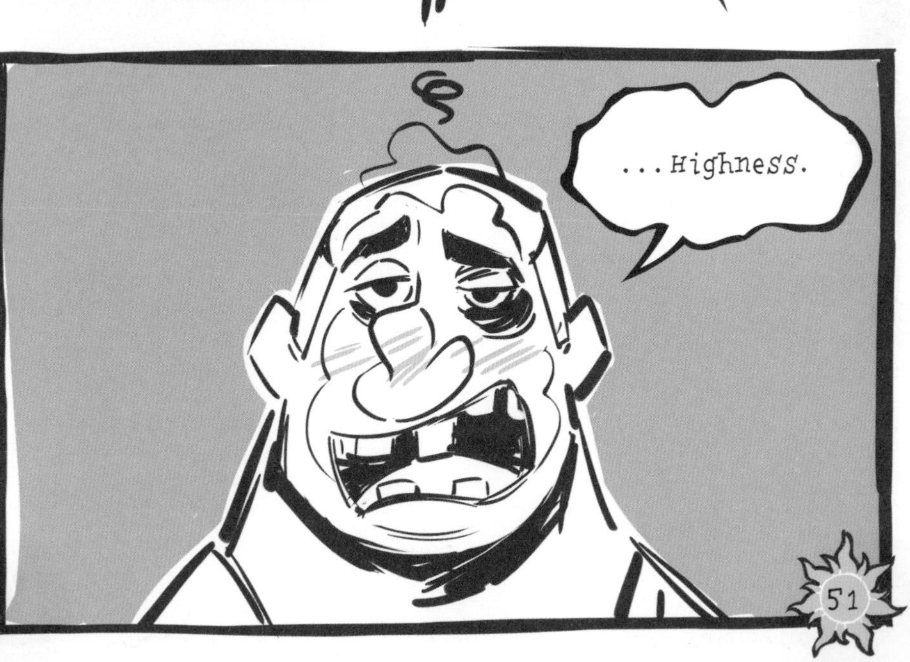
...Highness.

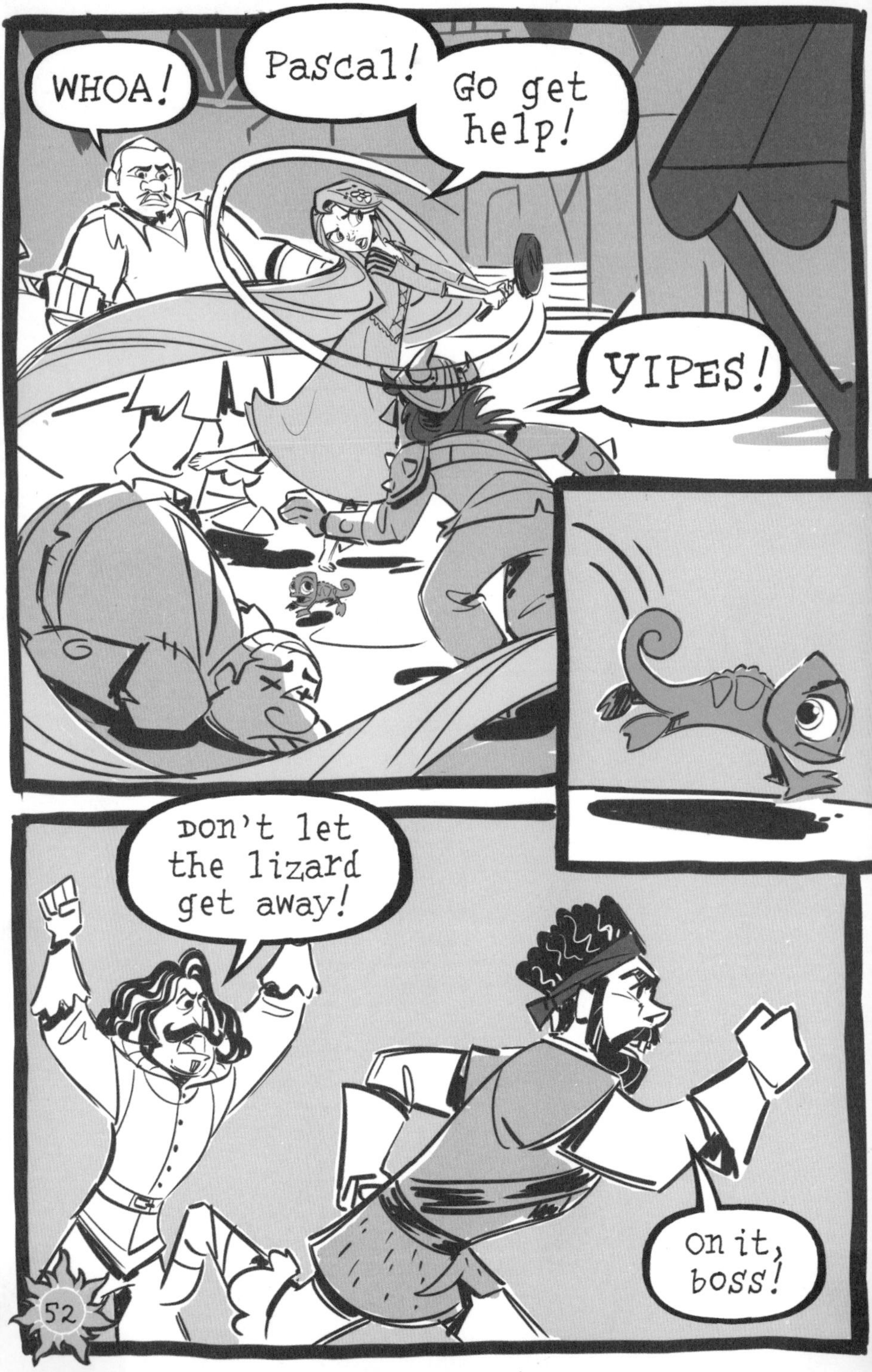
WHOA!
Pascal!
Go get help!
YIPES!
Don't let the lizard get away!
On it, boss!

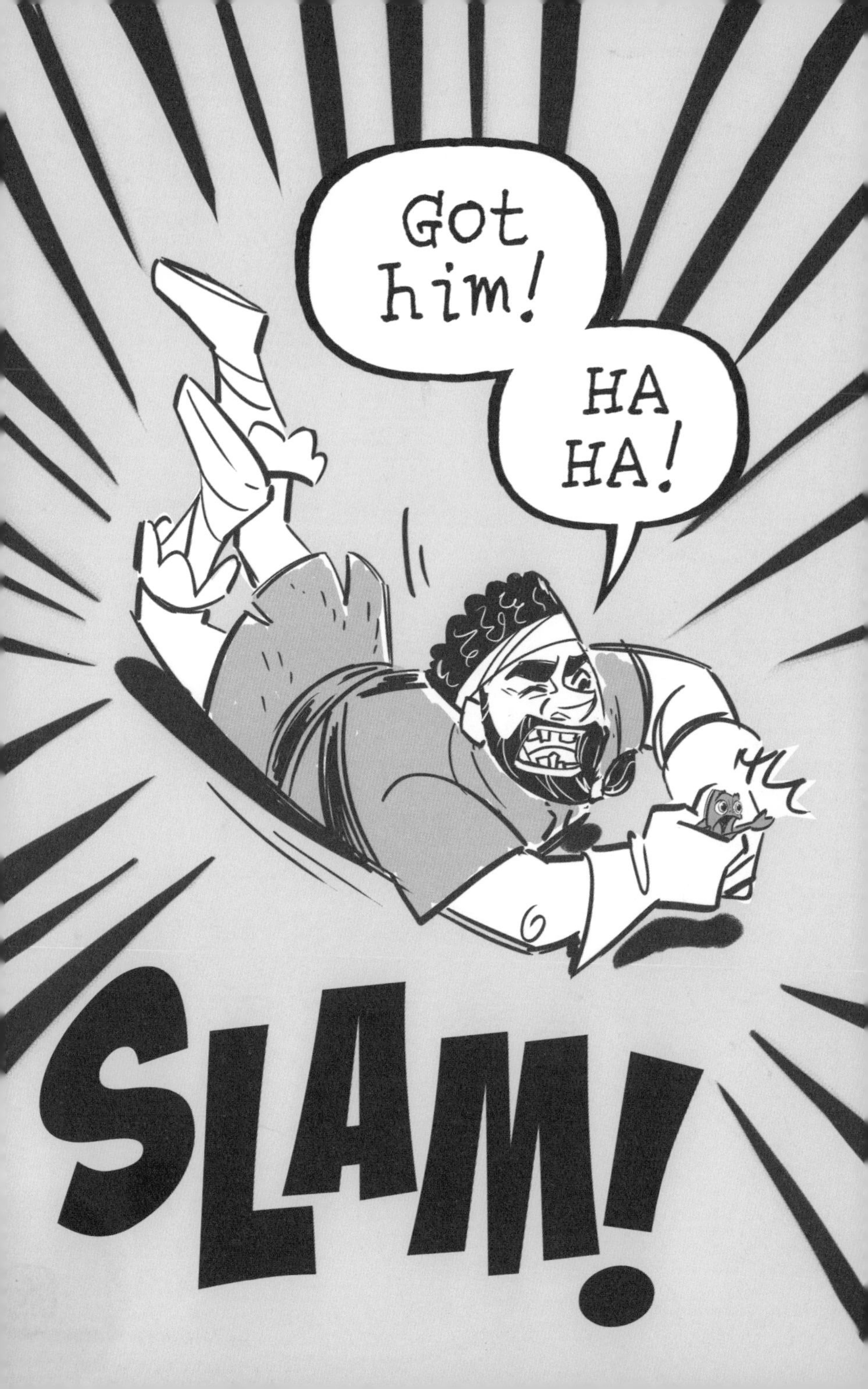
Got him!
HA HA!
SLAM!

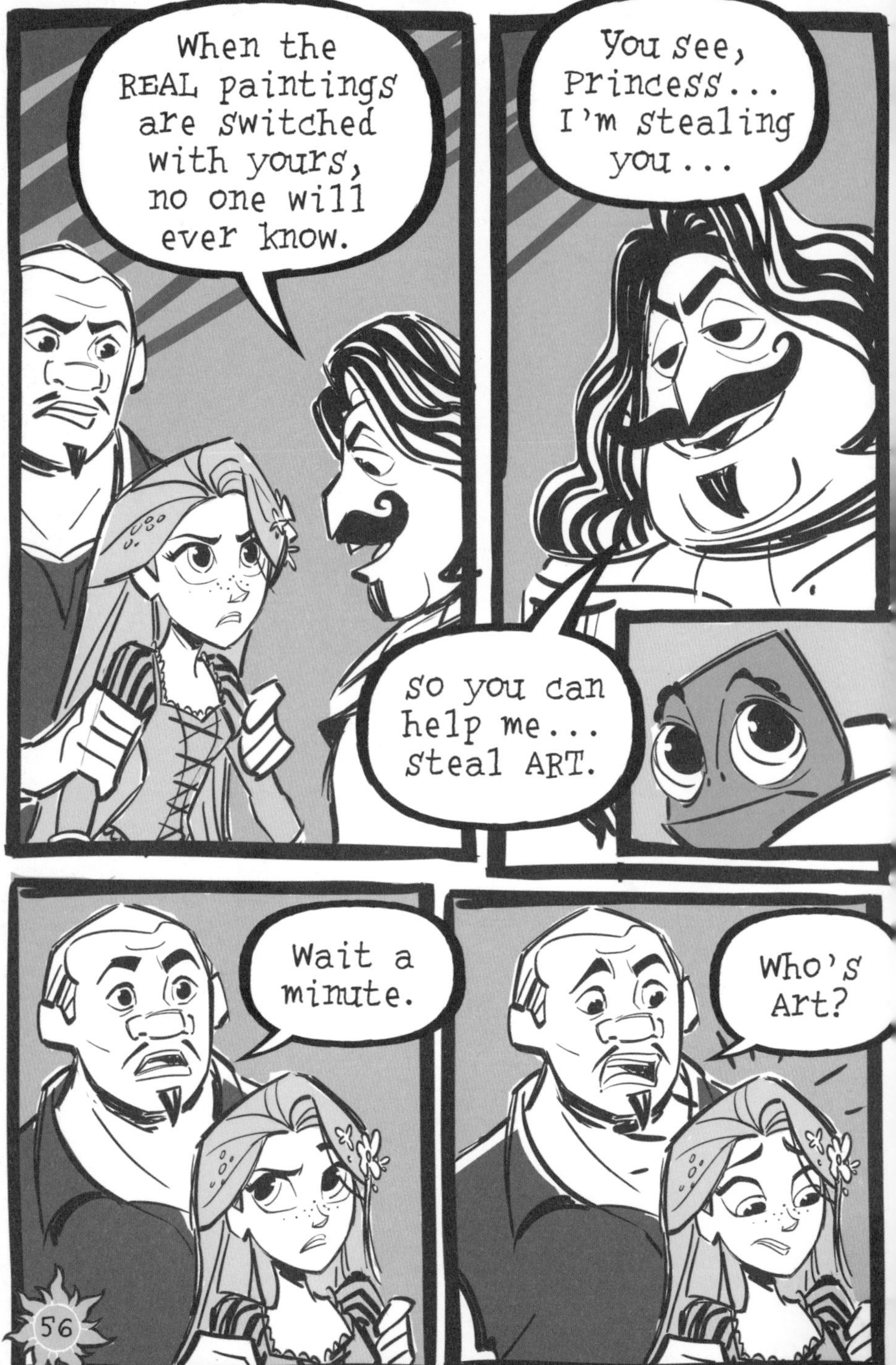
When the REAL paintings are switched with yours, no one will ever know.
You see, Princess... I'm stealing you...
so you can help me... steal ART.
Wait a minute.
Who's Art?

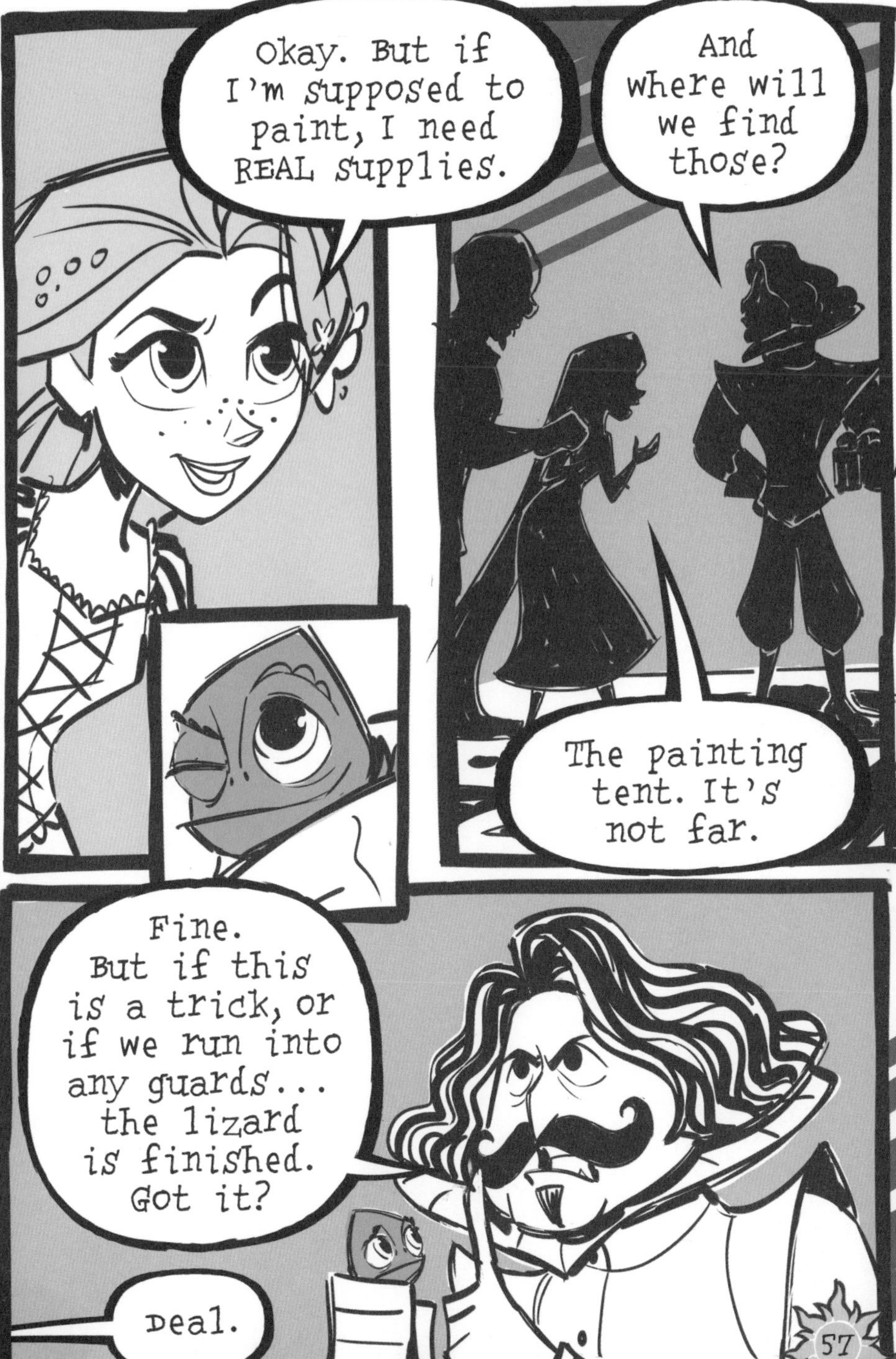
Okay. But if I'm supposed to paint, I need REAL supplies.
And where will we find those?
The painting tent. It's not far.
Fine. But if this is a trick, or if we run into any guards... the lizard is finished. Got it?
Deal.

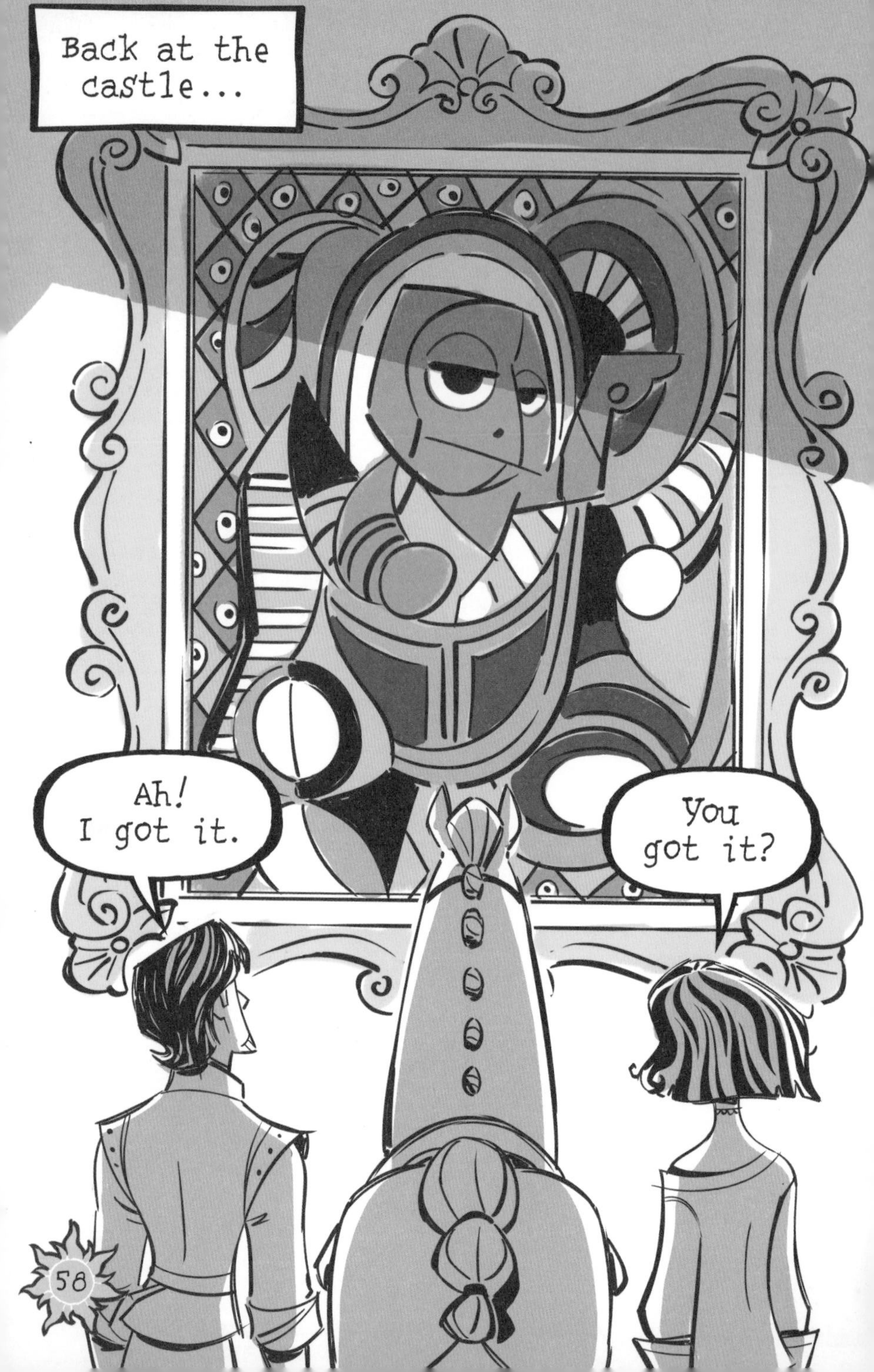
Back at the castle...
Ah! I got it.
You got it?

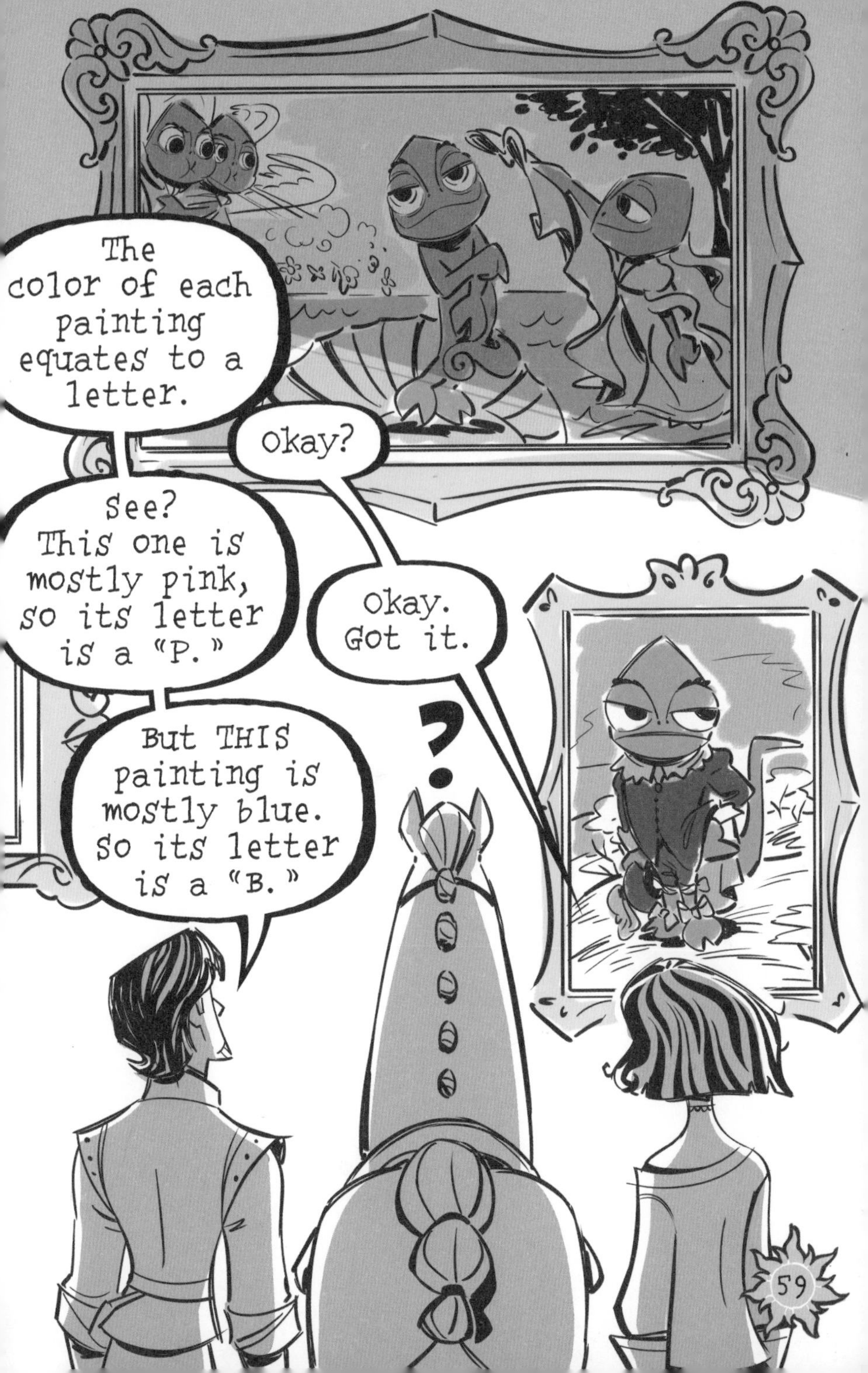

The color of each painting equates to a letter.
Okay?
See? This one is mostly pink, so its letter is a "P."
Okay. Got it.
But THIS painting is mostly blue. So its letter is a "B."
?

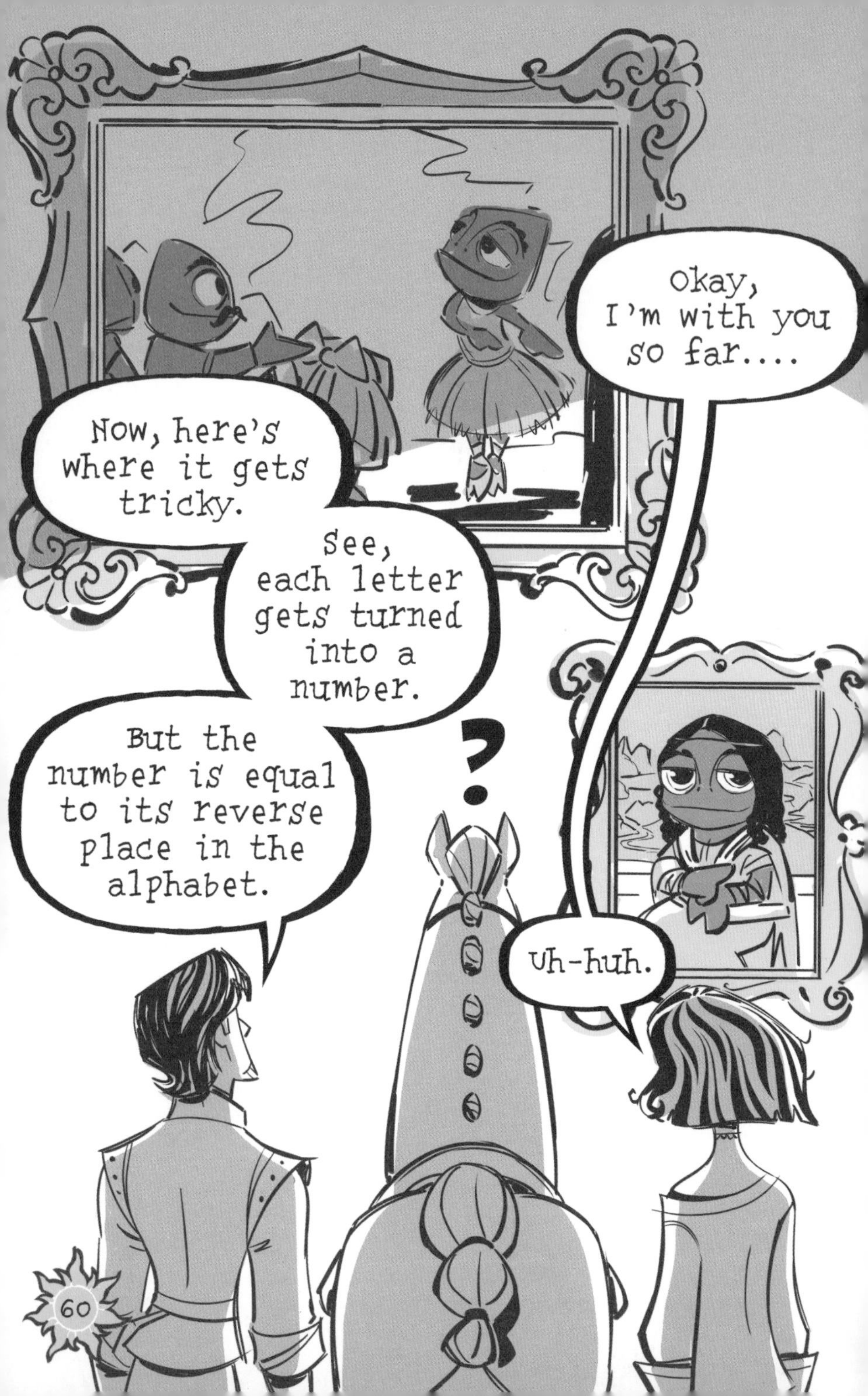
Now, here's where it gets tricky.
Okay, I'm with you so far....
See, each letter gets turned into a number.
But the number is equal to its reverse place in the alphabet.
?
Uh-huh.

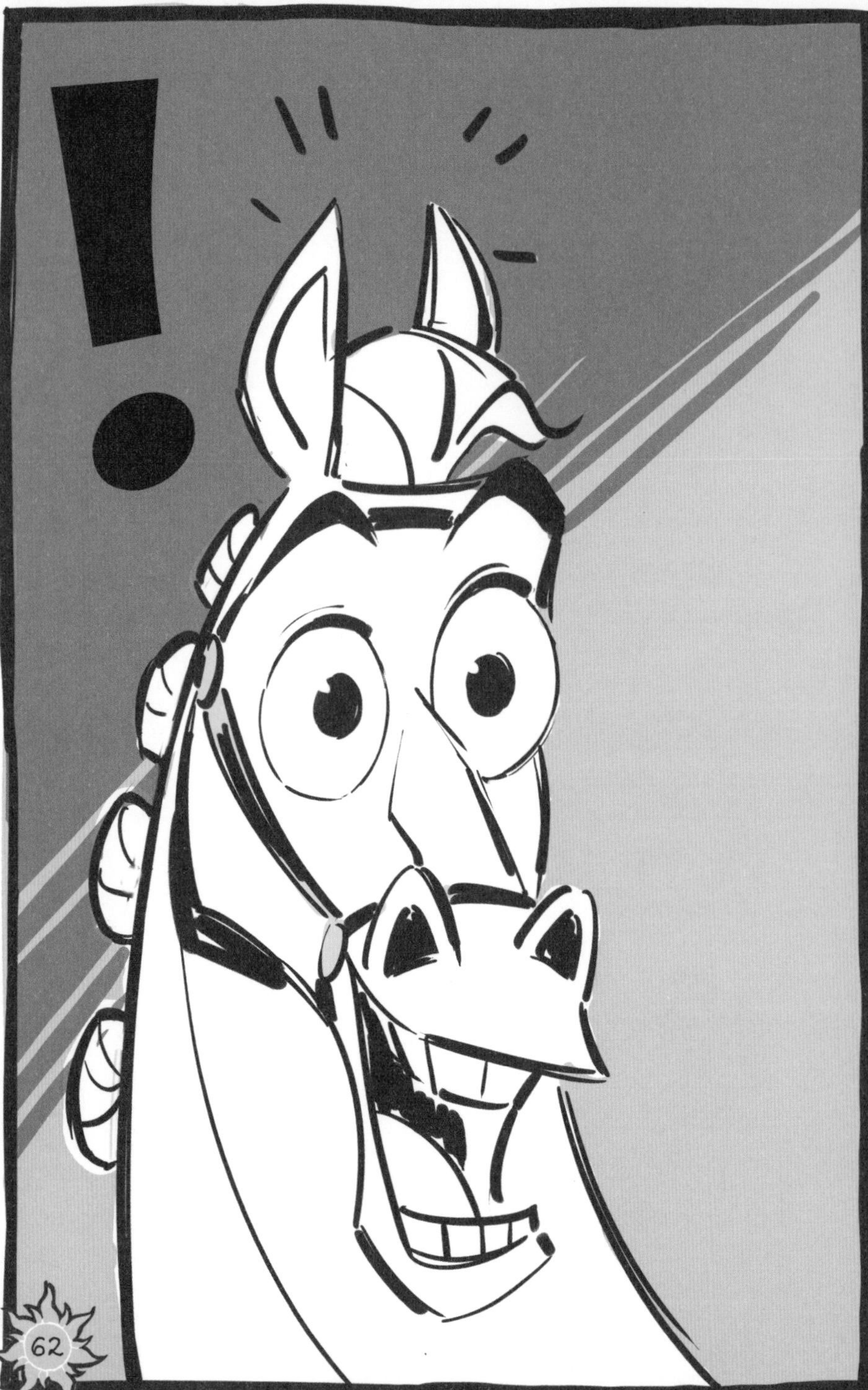
!

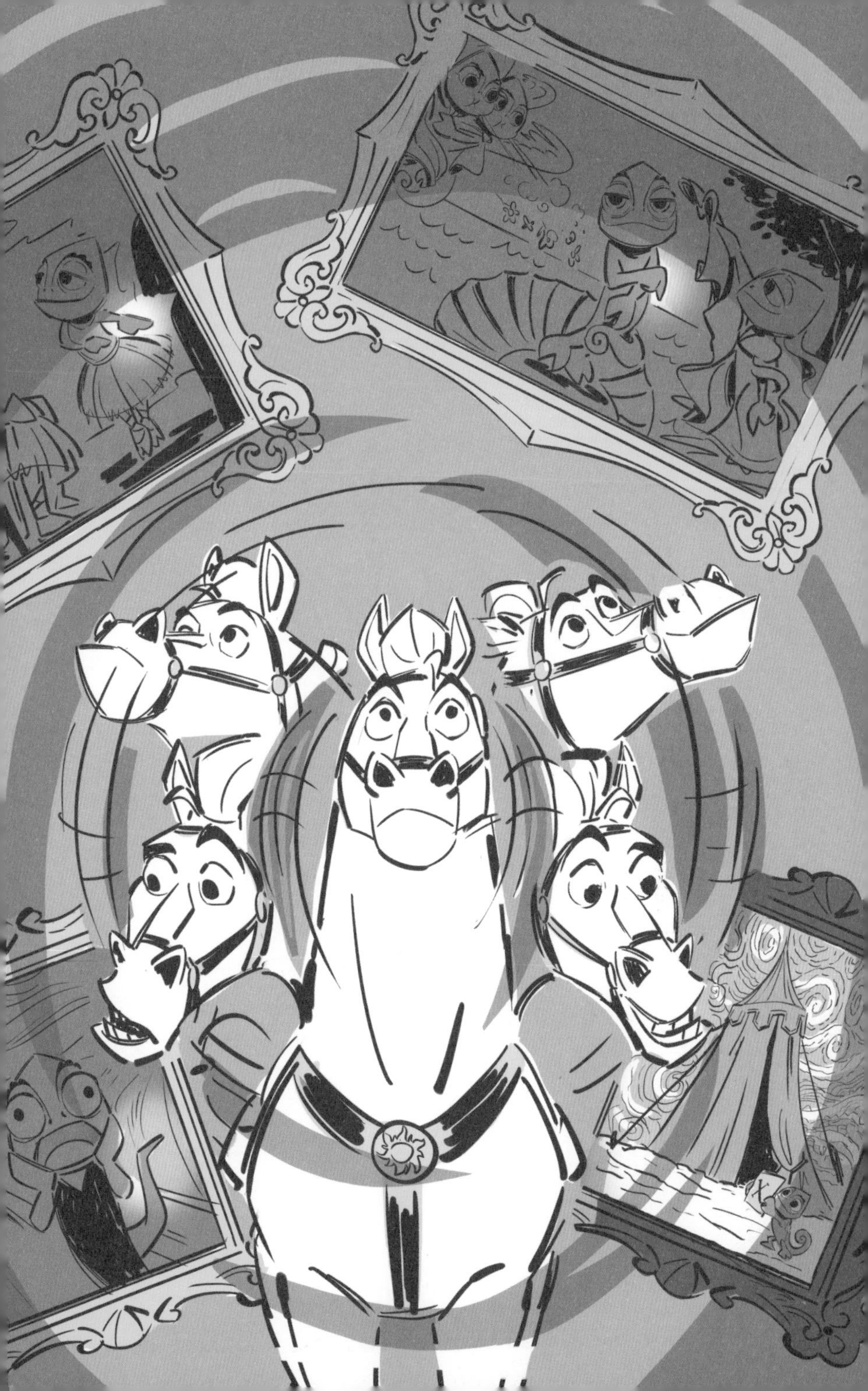

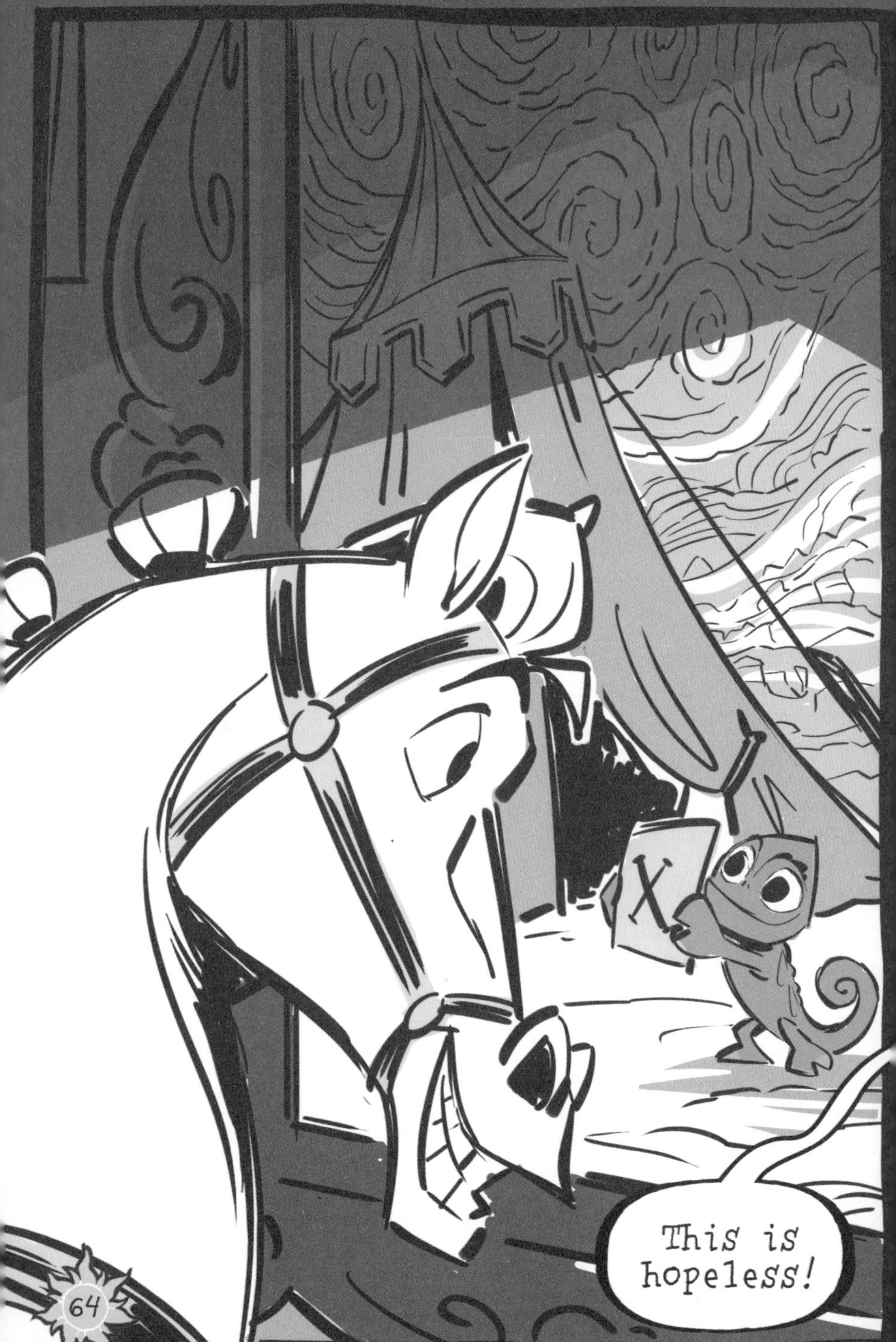
X
This is hopeless!

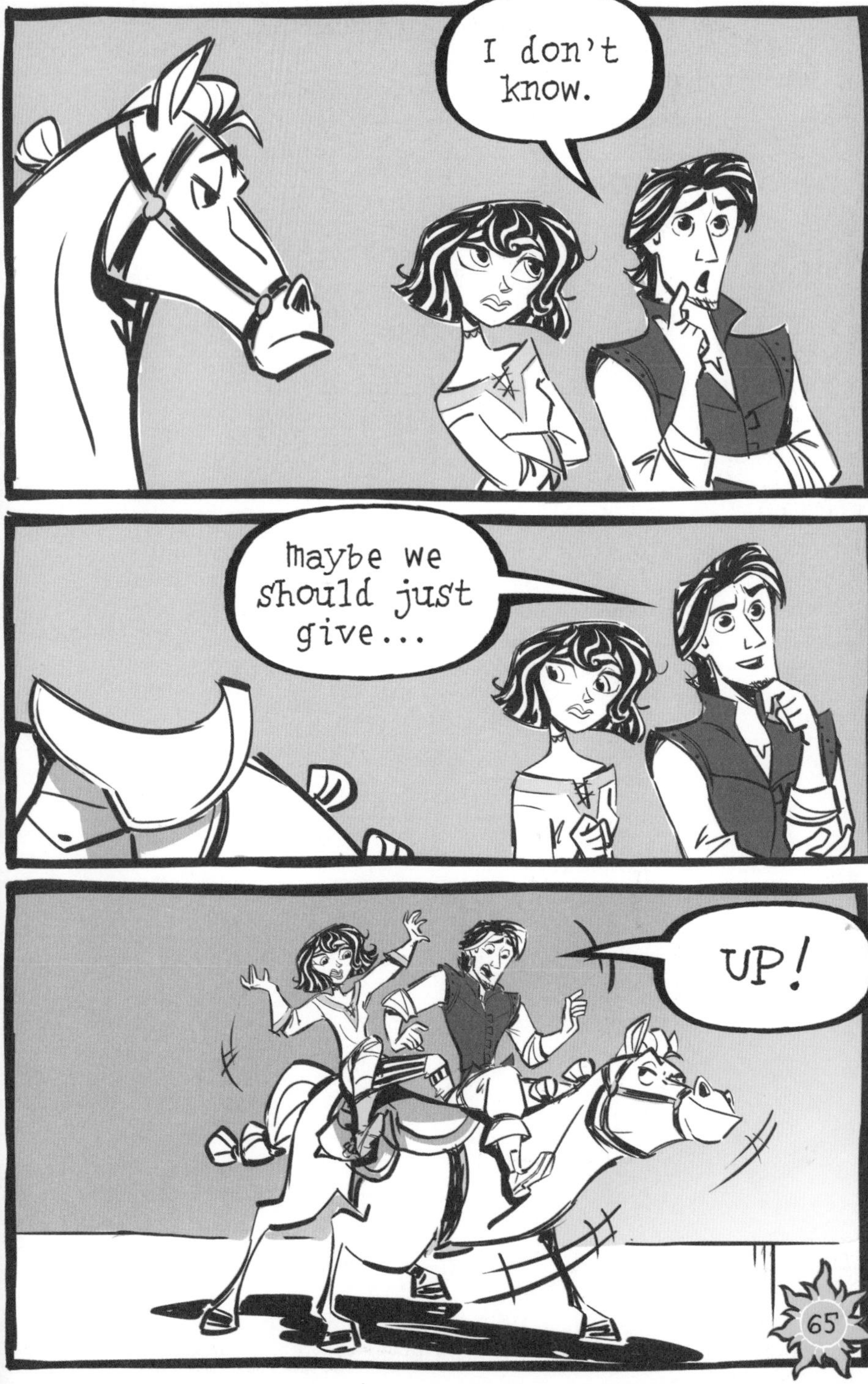
I don't know.
maybe we should just give...
UP!

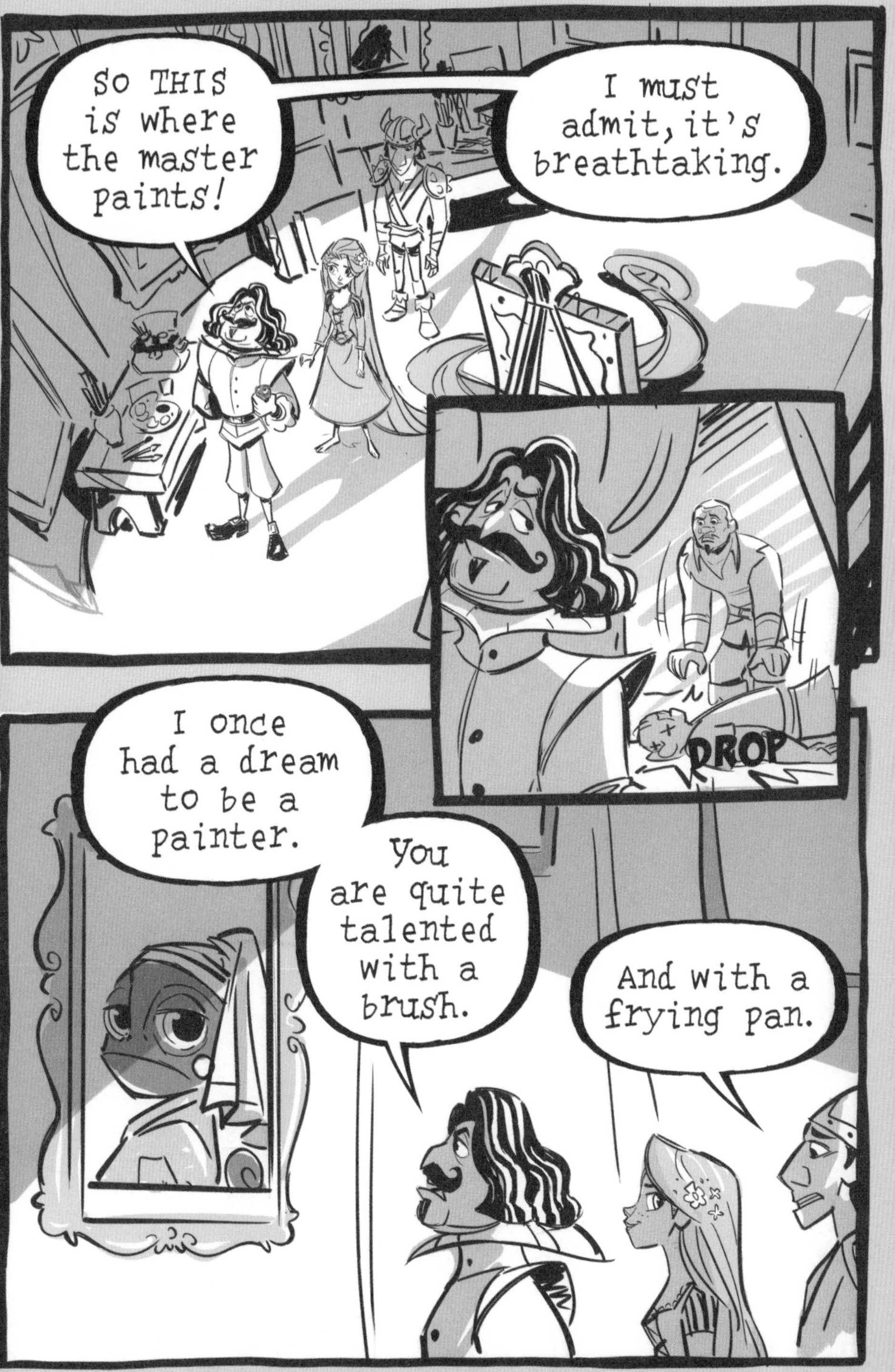
SO THIS is where the master paints!
I must admit, it's breathtaking.
DROP
I once had a dream to be a painter.
You are quite talented with a brush.
And with a frying pan.

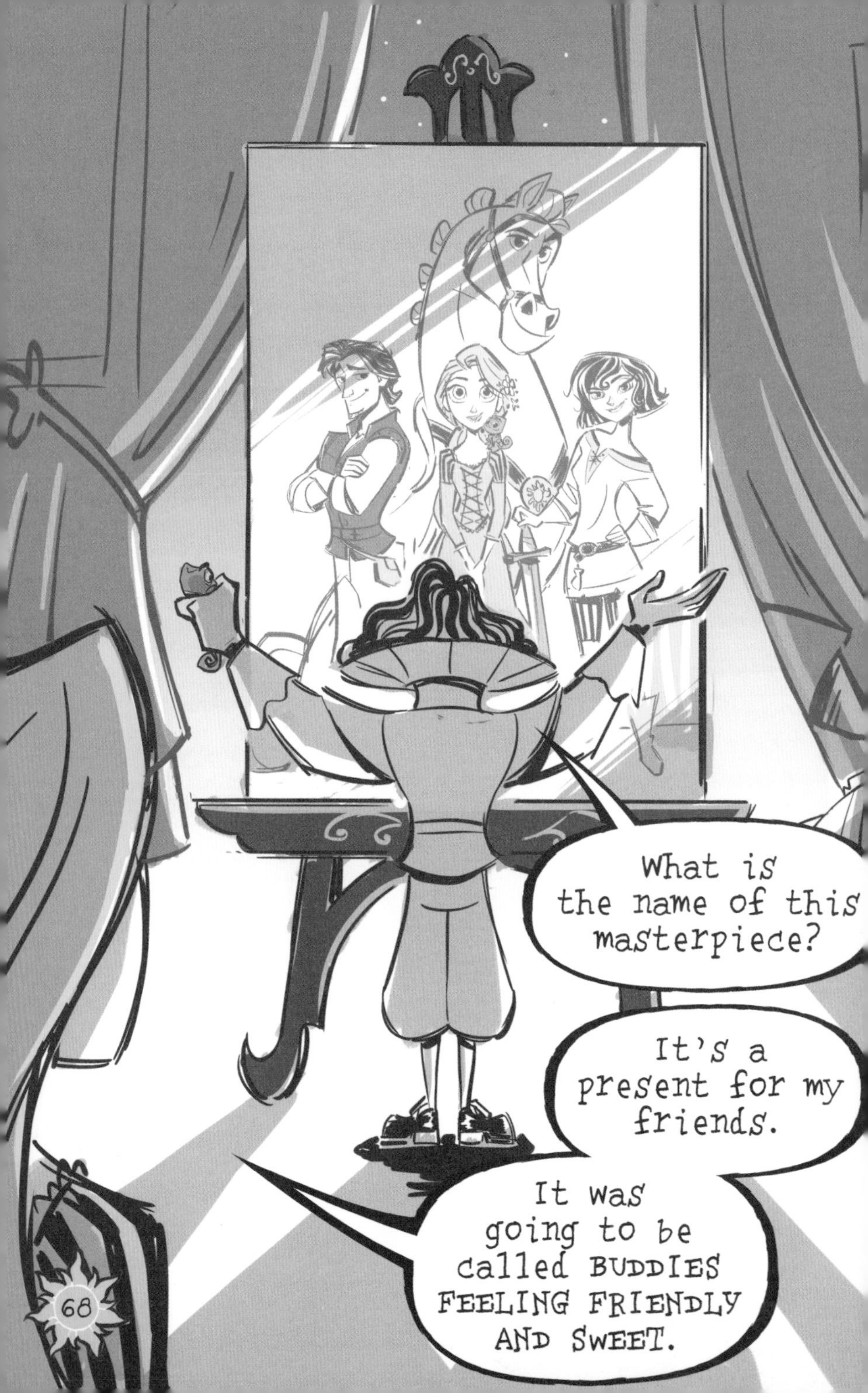
What is the name of this masterpiece?
It's a present for my friends.
It was going to be called BUDDIES FEELING FRIENDLY AND SWEET.

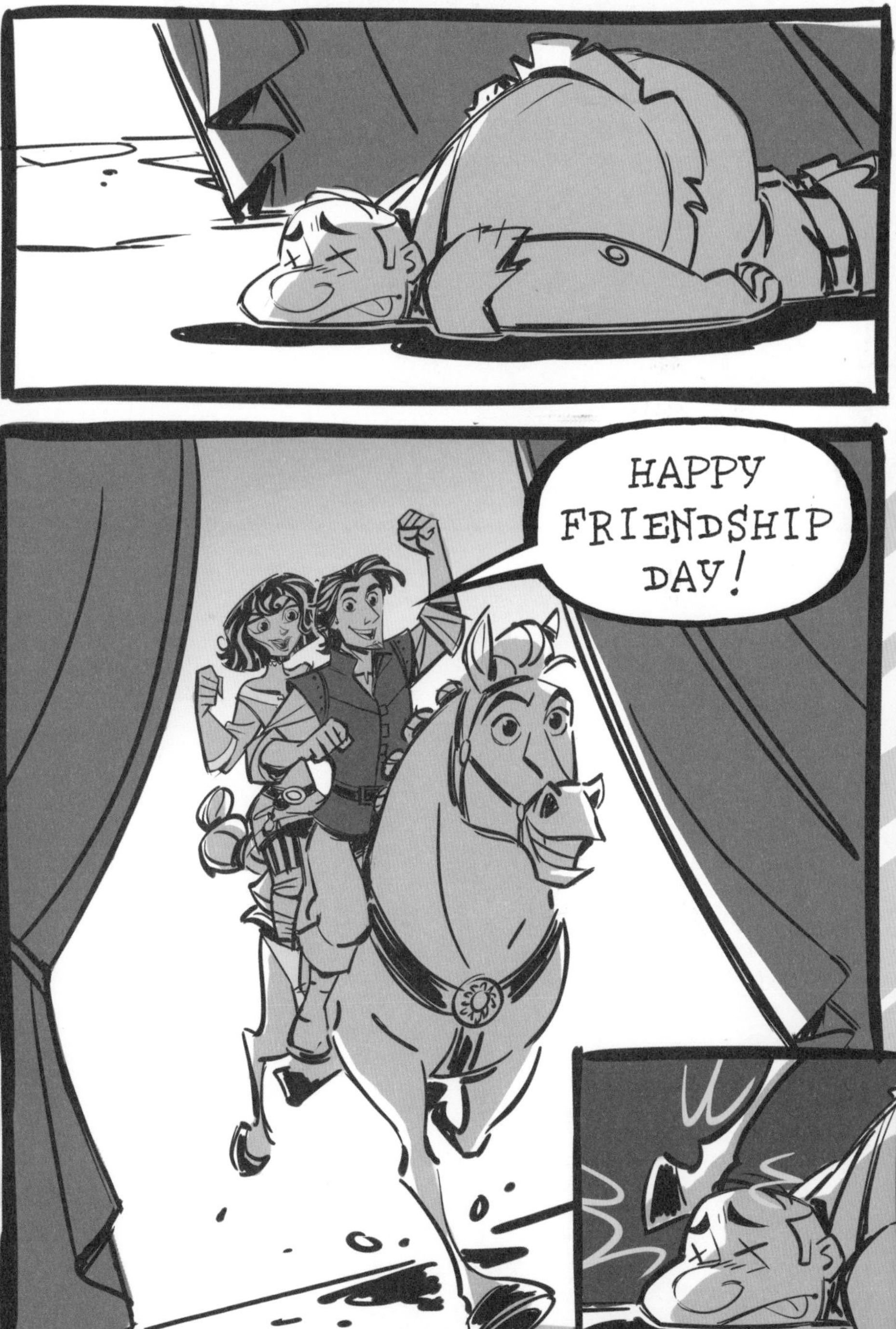
HAPPY FRIENDSHIP DAY!

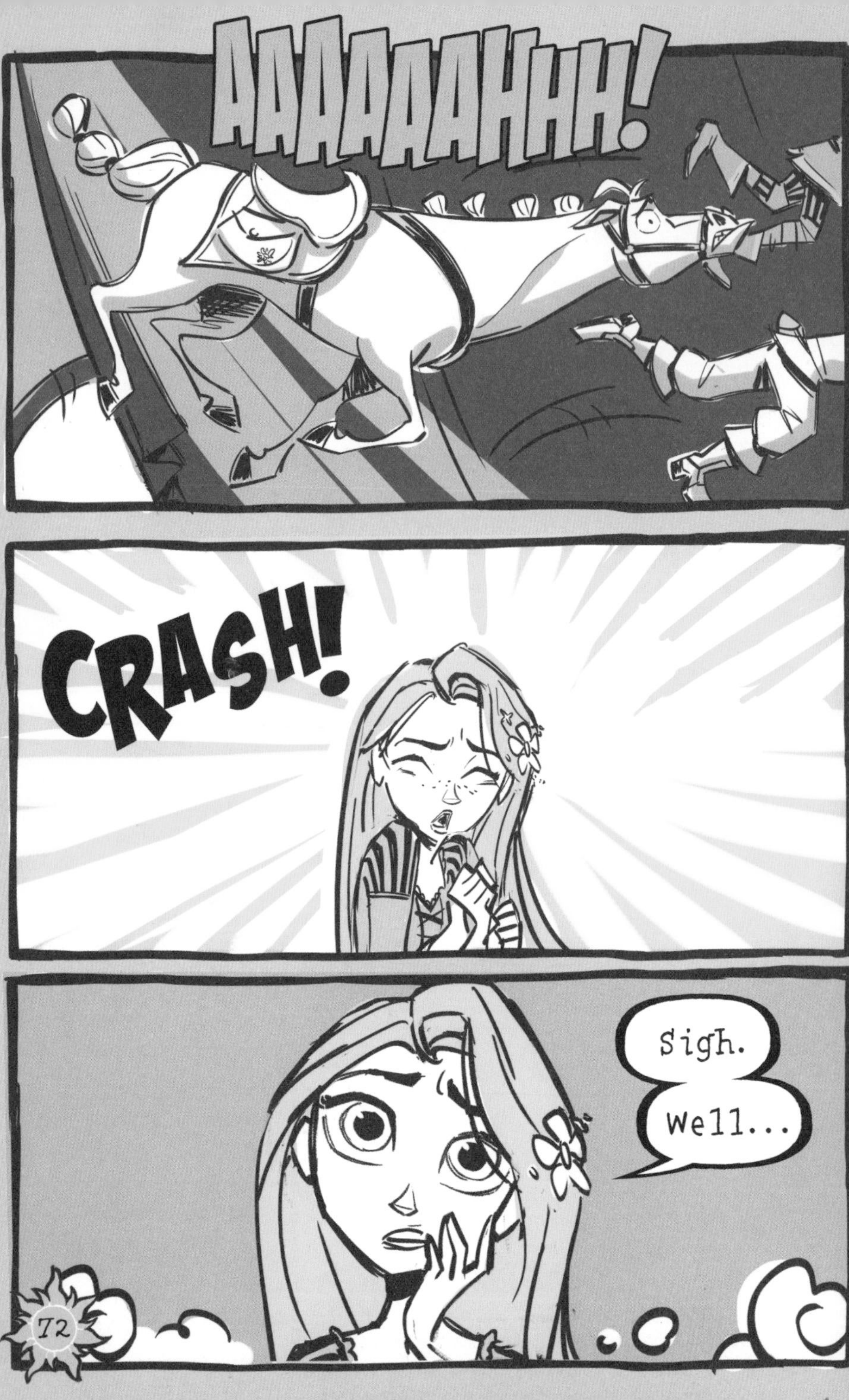
AAAAAAHHH!
CRASH!
Sigh.
Well...

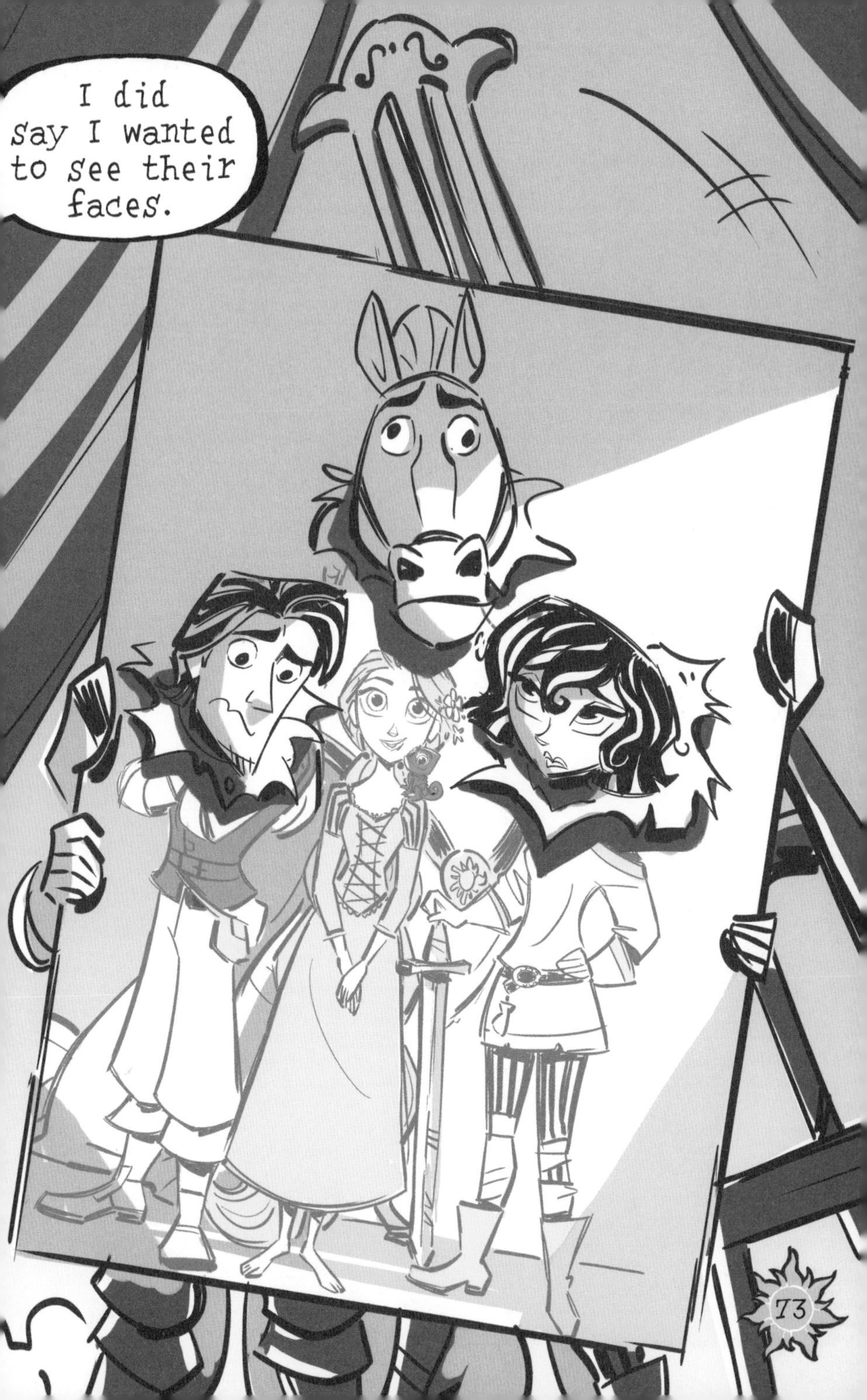
I did say I wanted to see their faces.

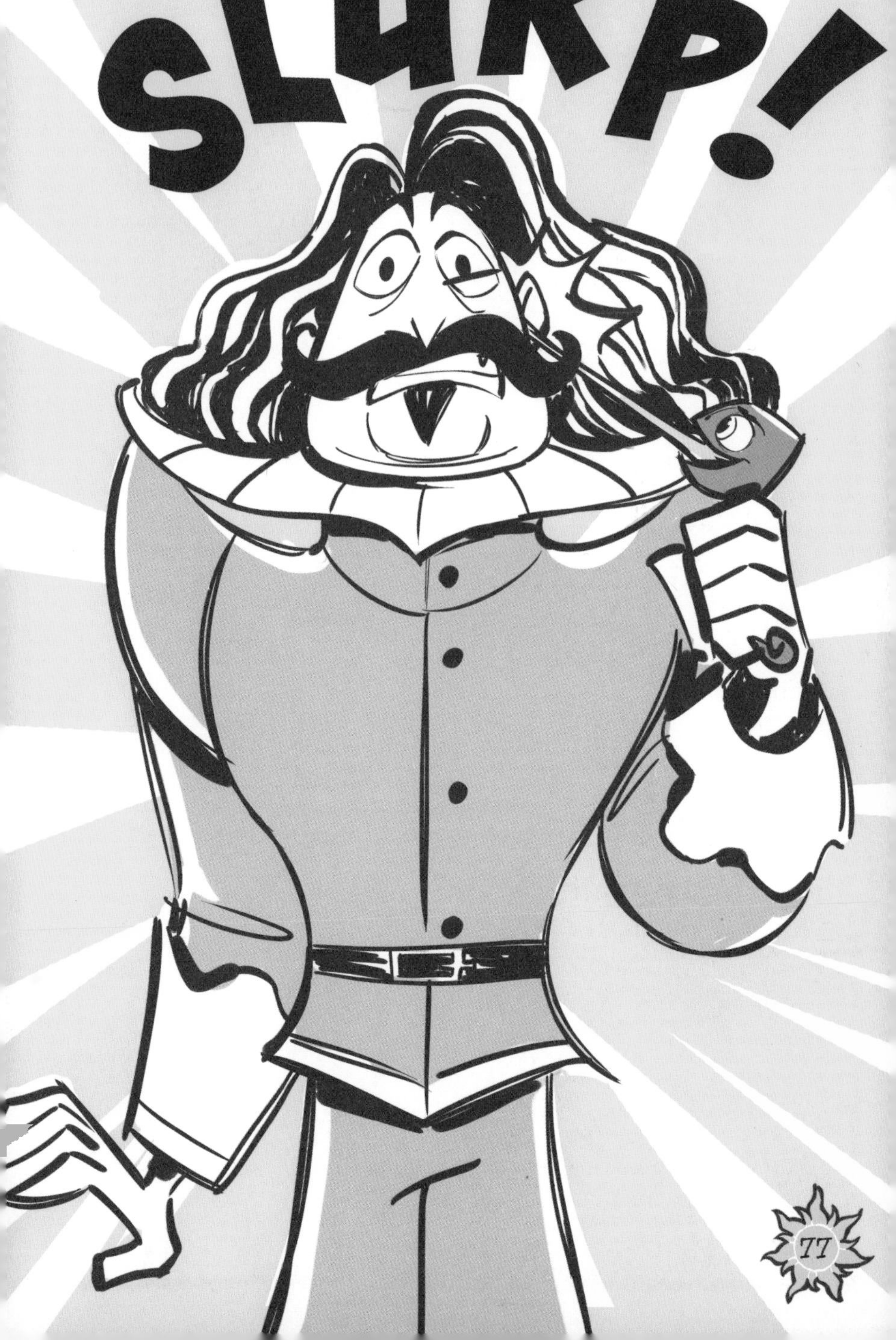
SLURP!

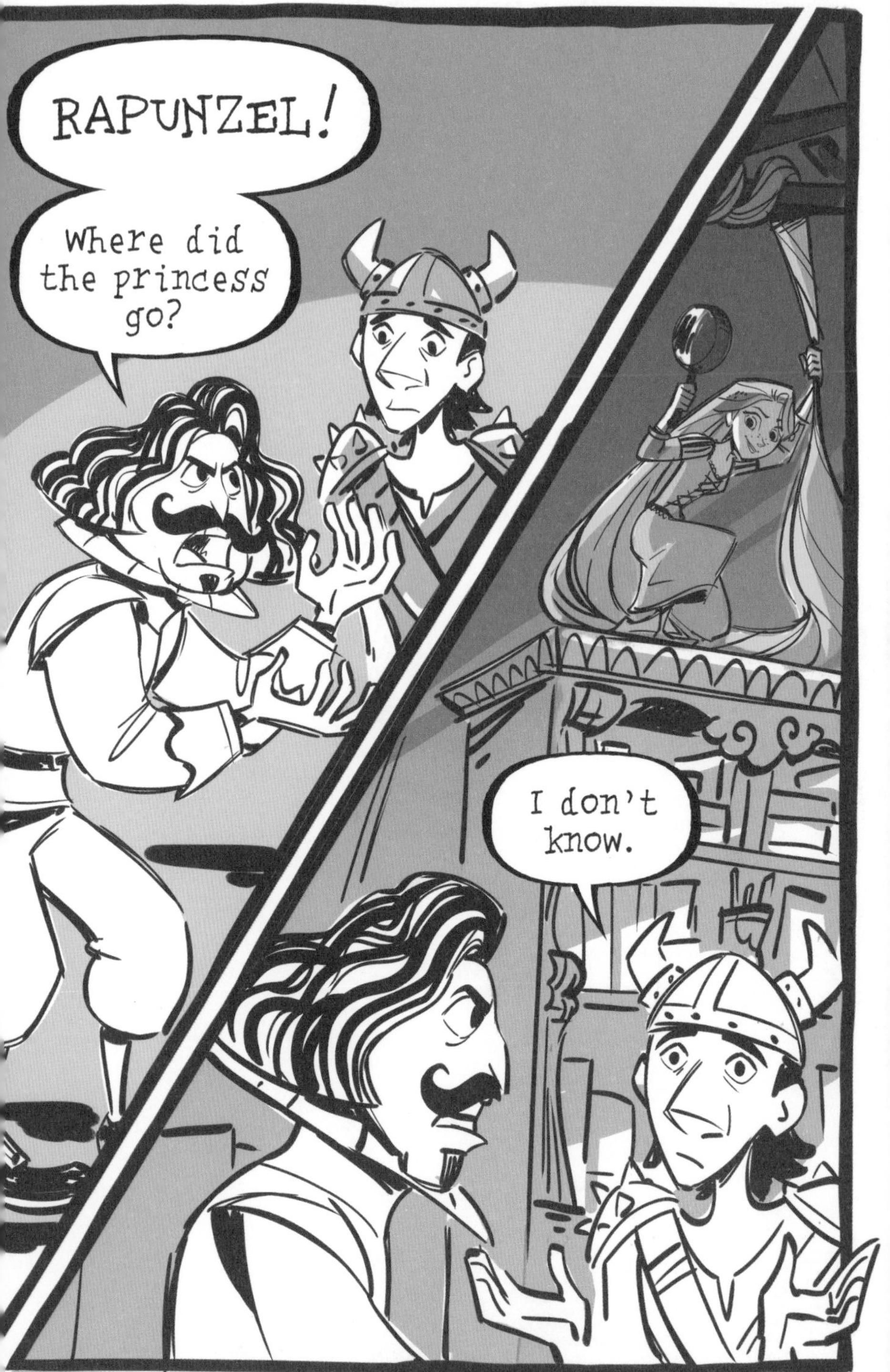
RAPUNZEL!
Where did the princess go?
I don't know.

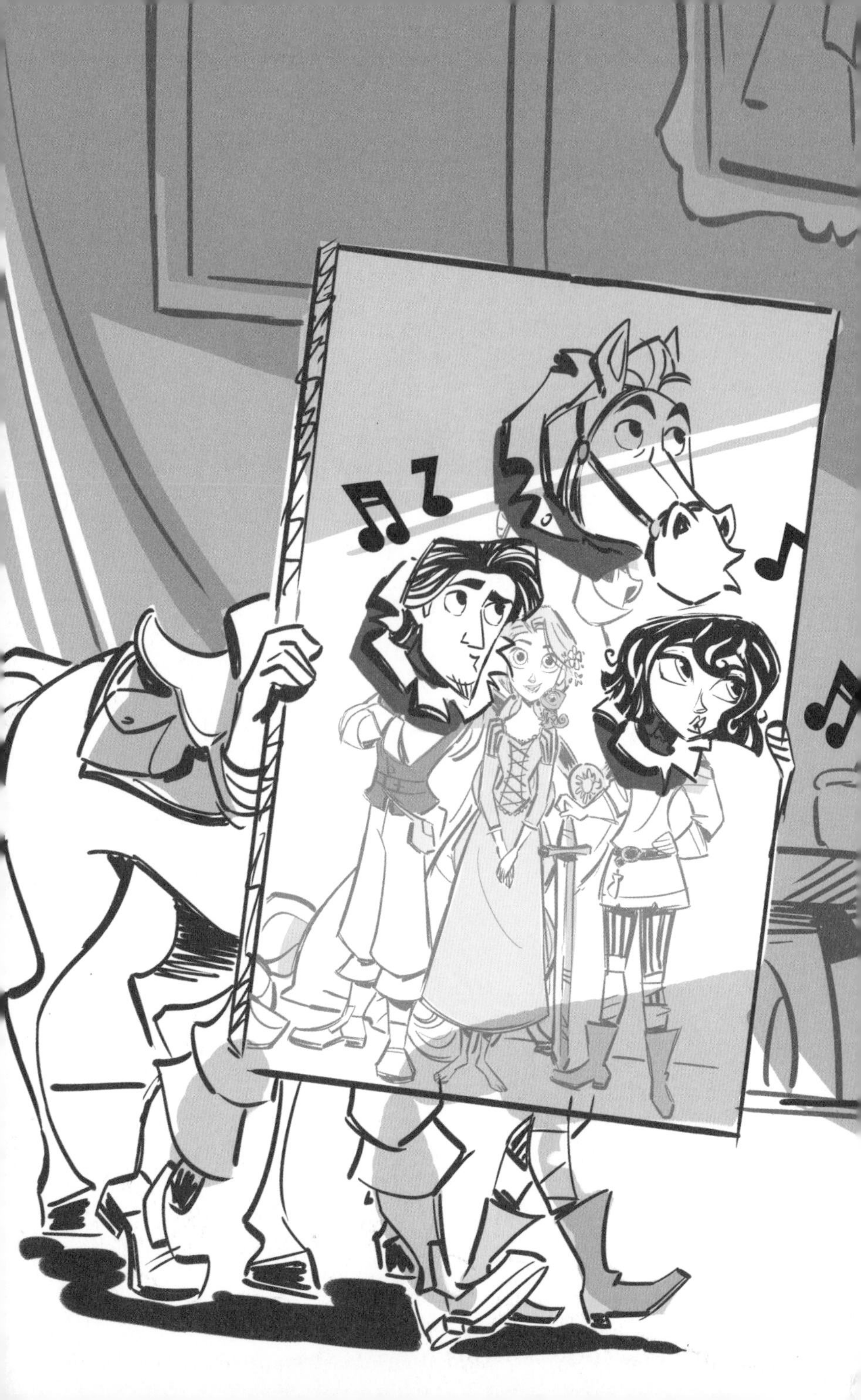

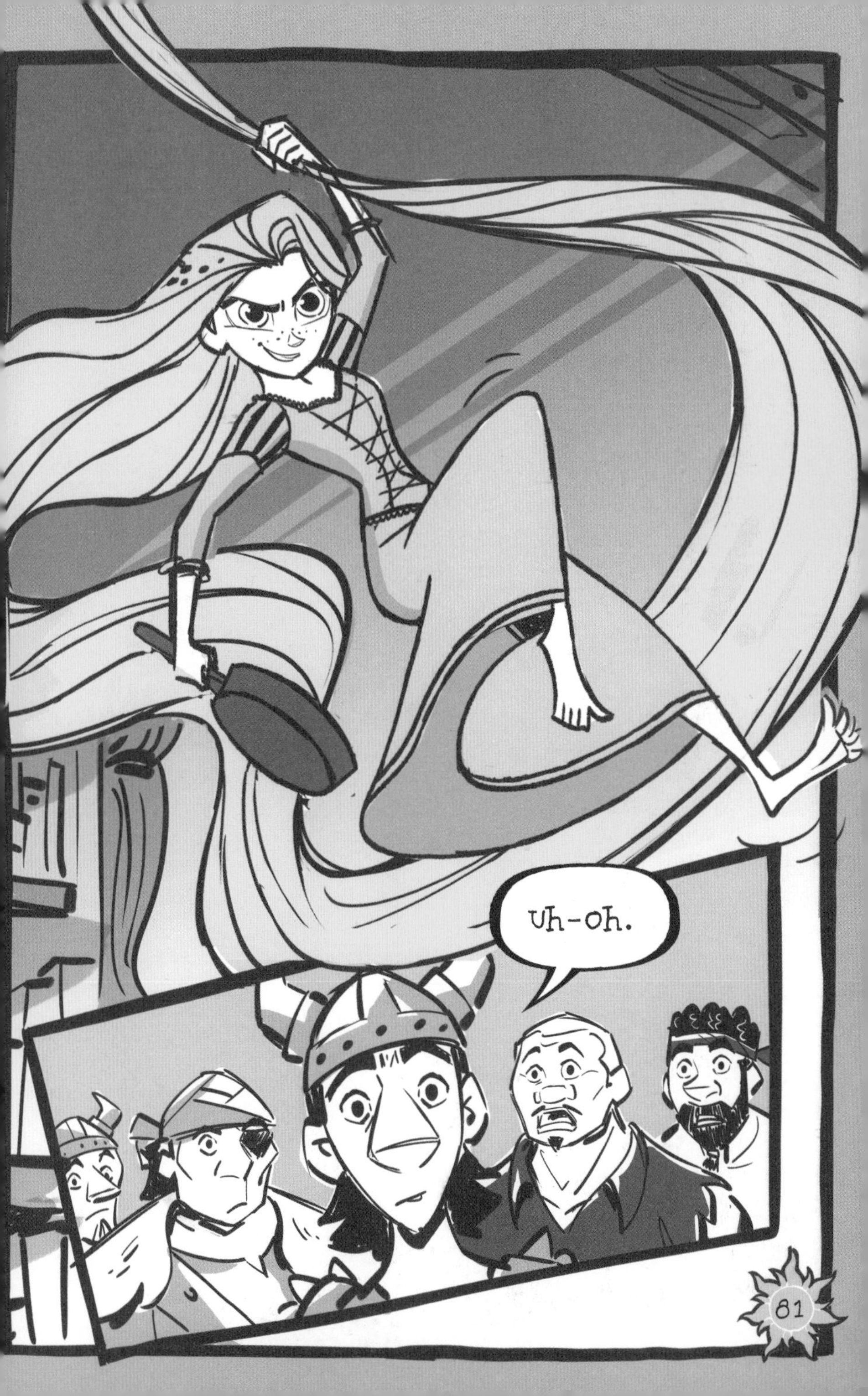
Uh-oh.

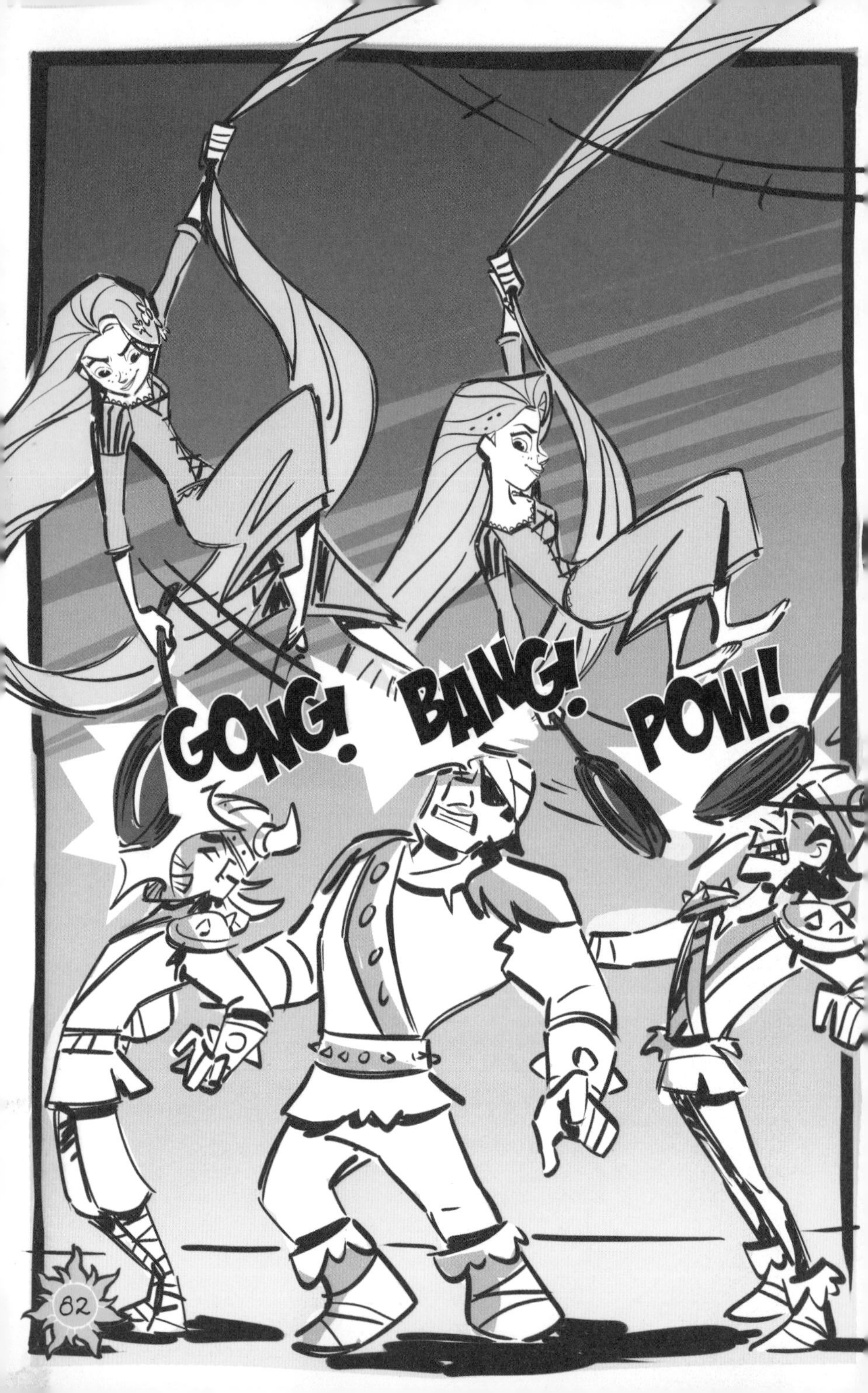
GONG!
BANG!
POW!

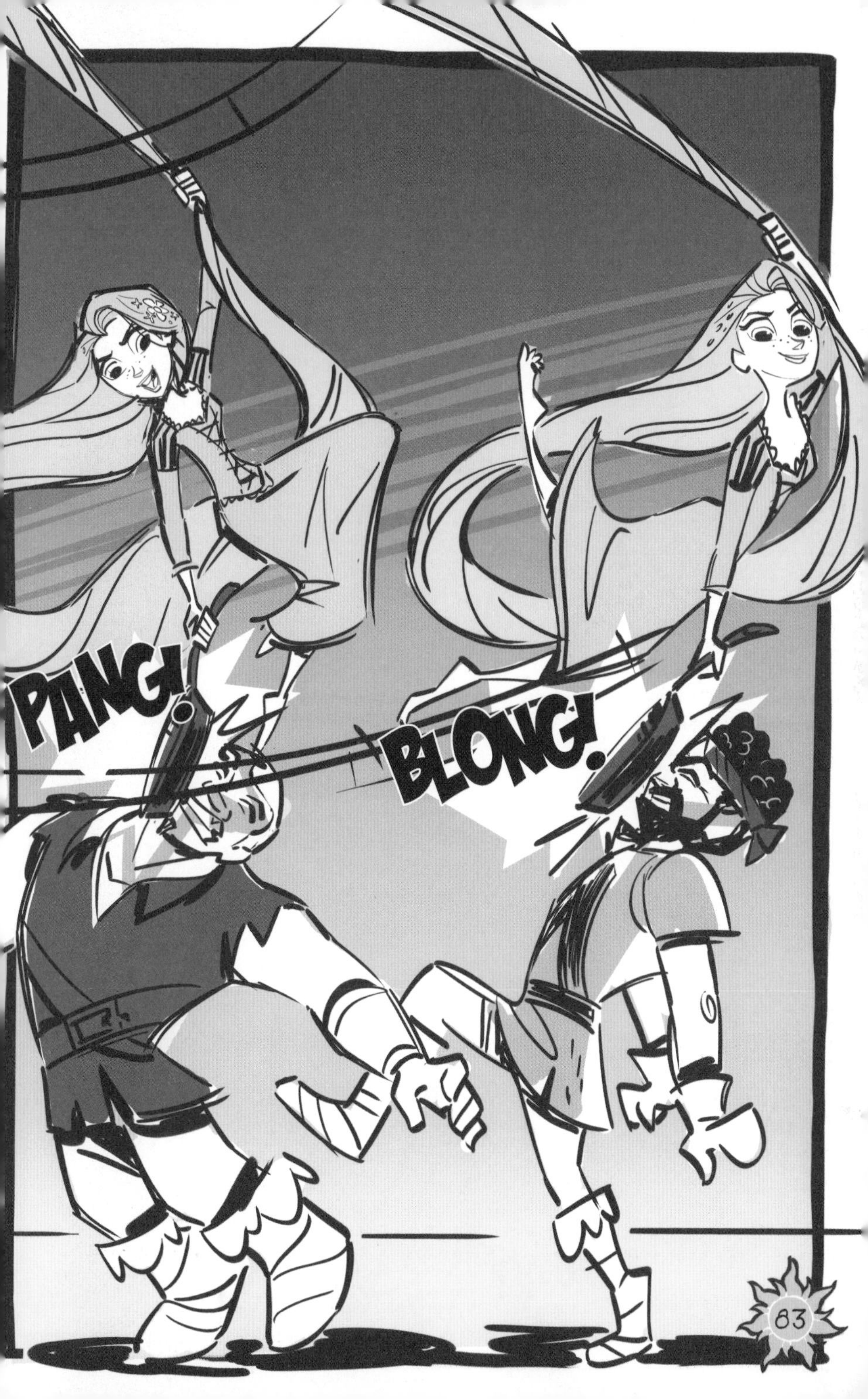
PANG!
BLONG!

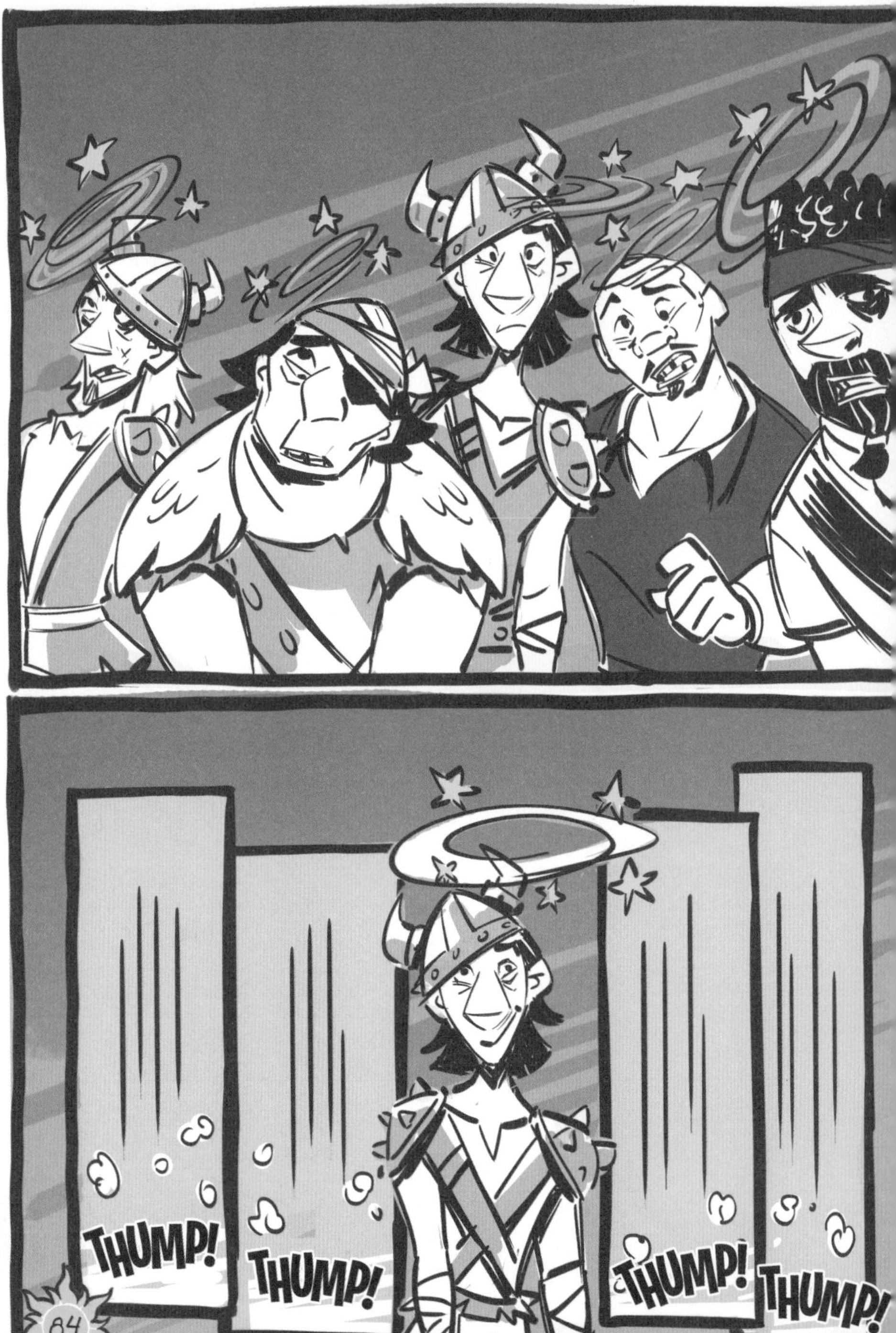
THUMP!
THUMP!
THUMP!
THUMP!

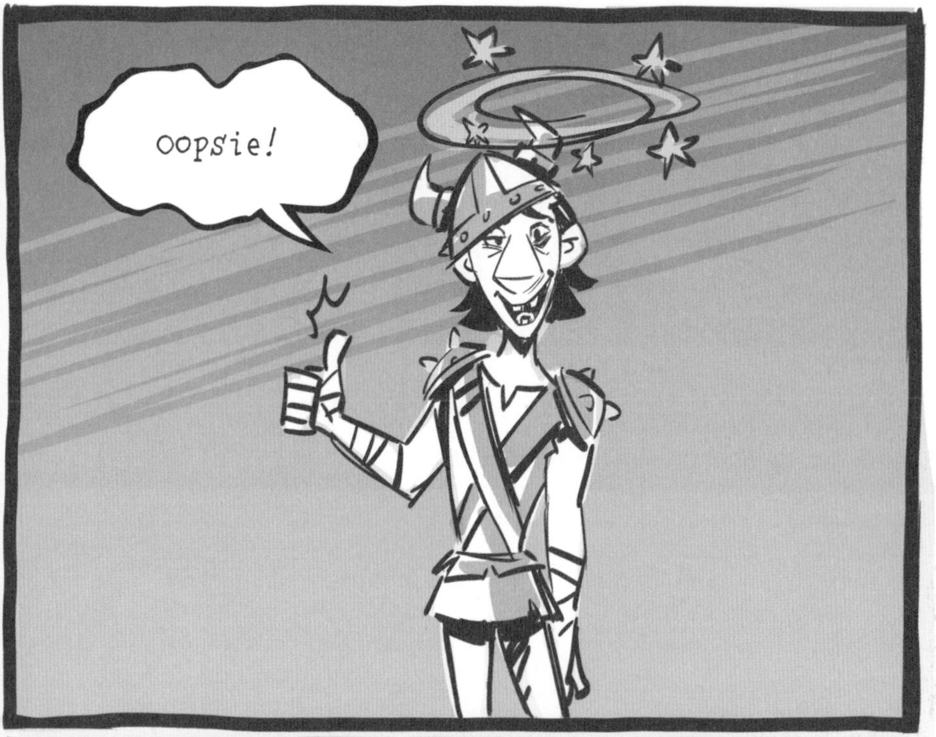
oopsie!
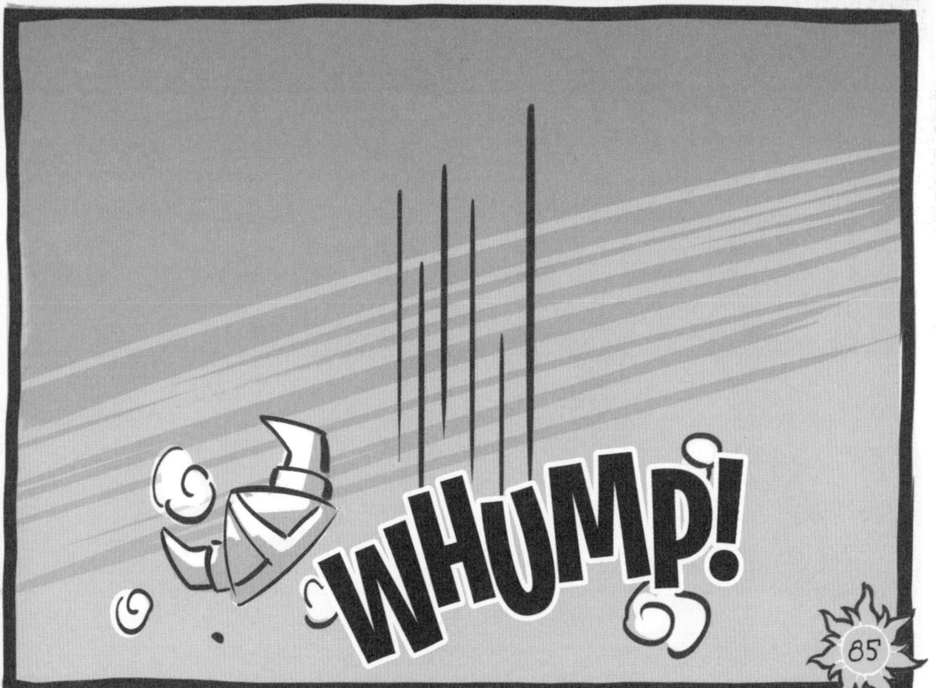
WHUMP!

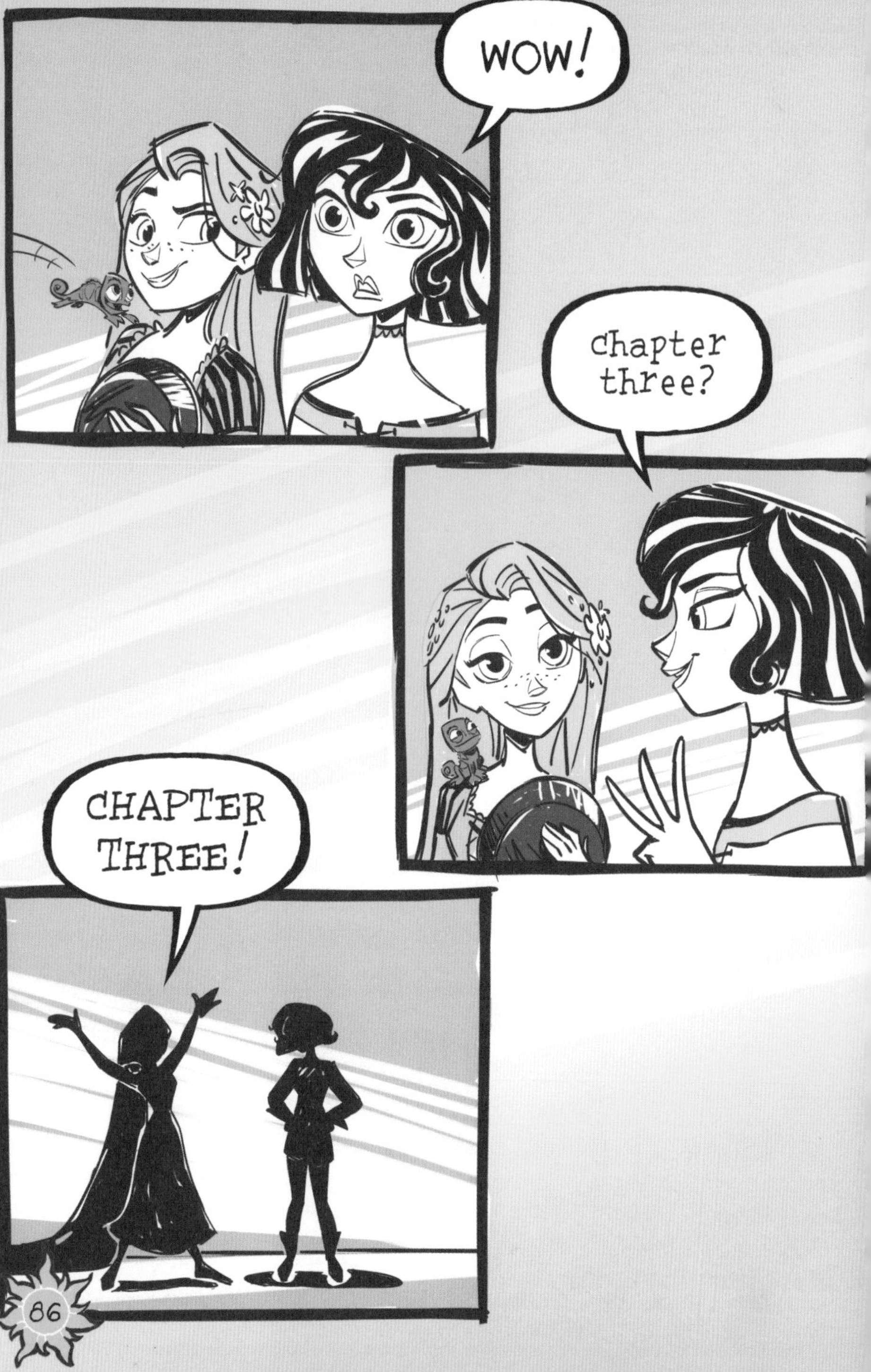
WOW!
chapter three?
CHAPTER THREE!

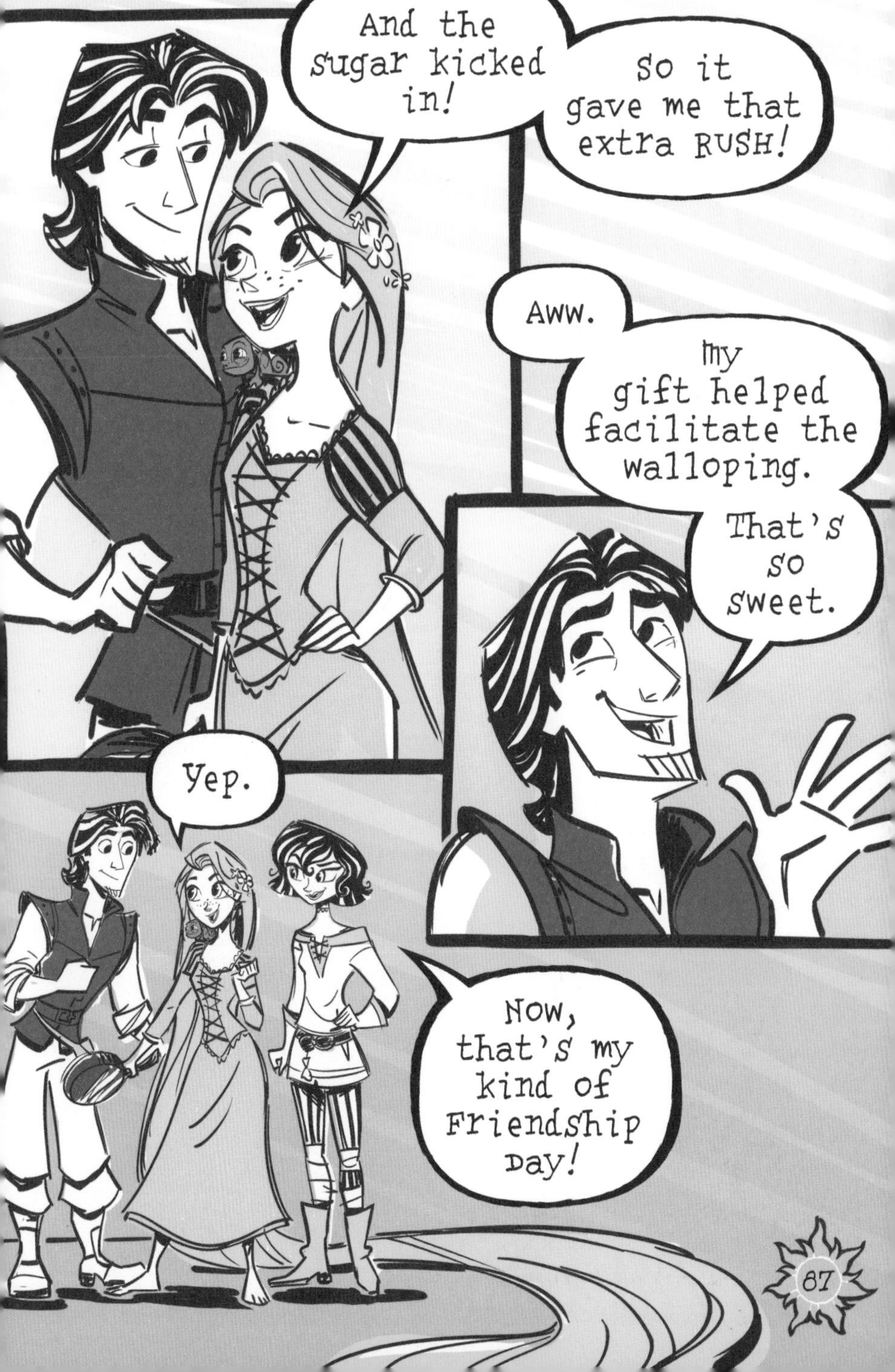
And the sugar kicked in!
So it gave me that extra RUSH!
Aww.
My gift helped facilitate the walloping.
That's so sweet.
Yep.
Now, that's my kind of Friendship Day!

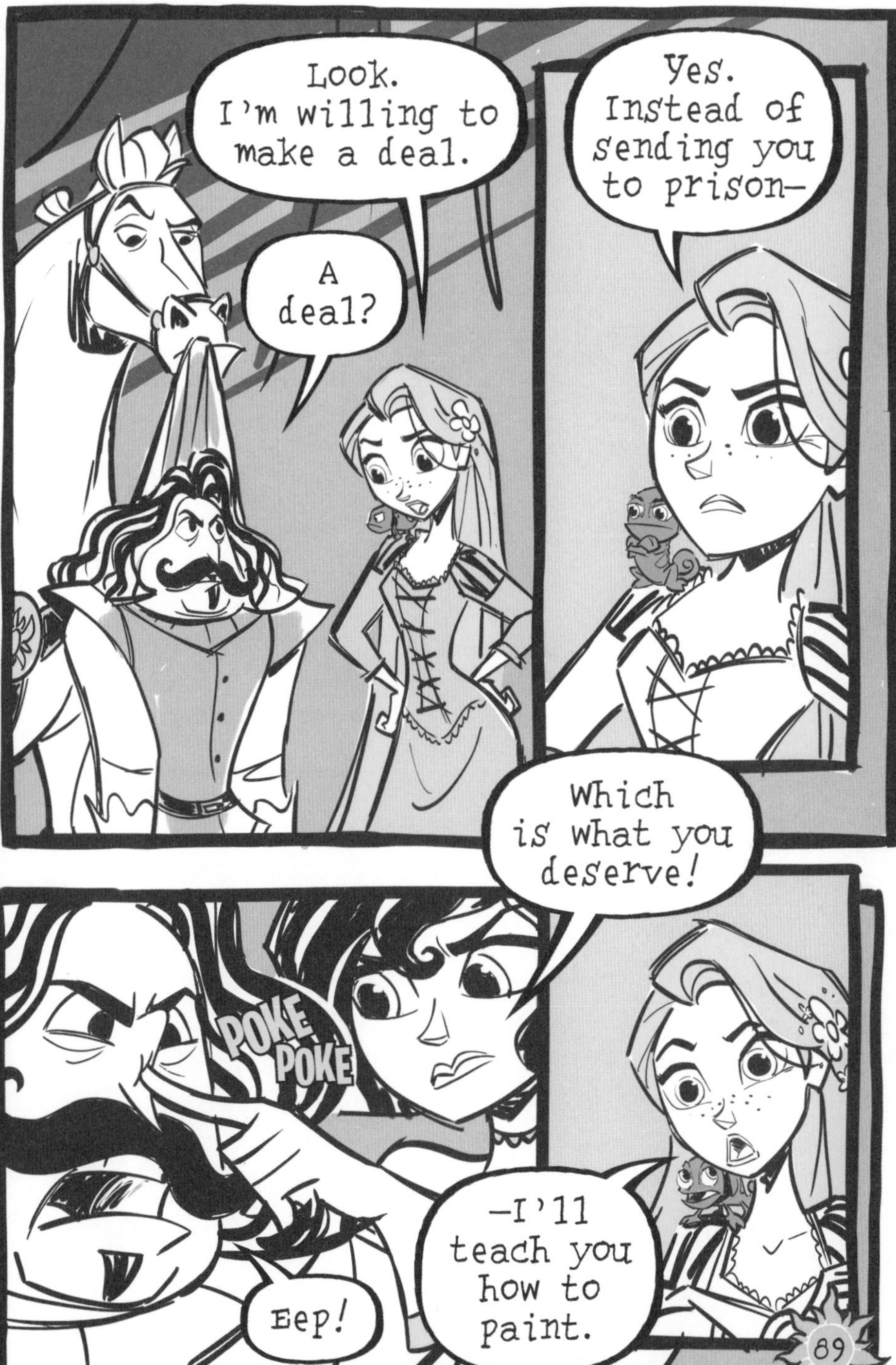
Look. I'm willing to make a deal.
A deal?
Yes. Instead of sending you to prison—
Which is what you deserve!
POKE POKE
Eep!
—I'll teach you how to paint.

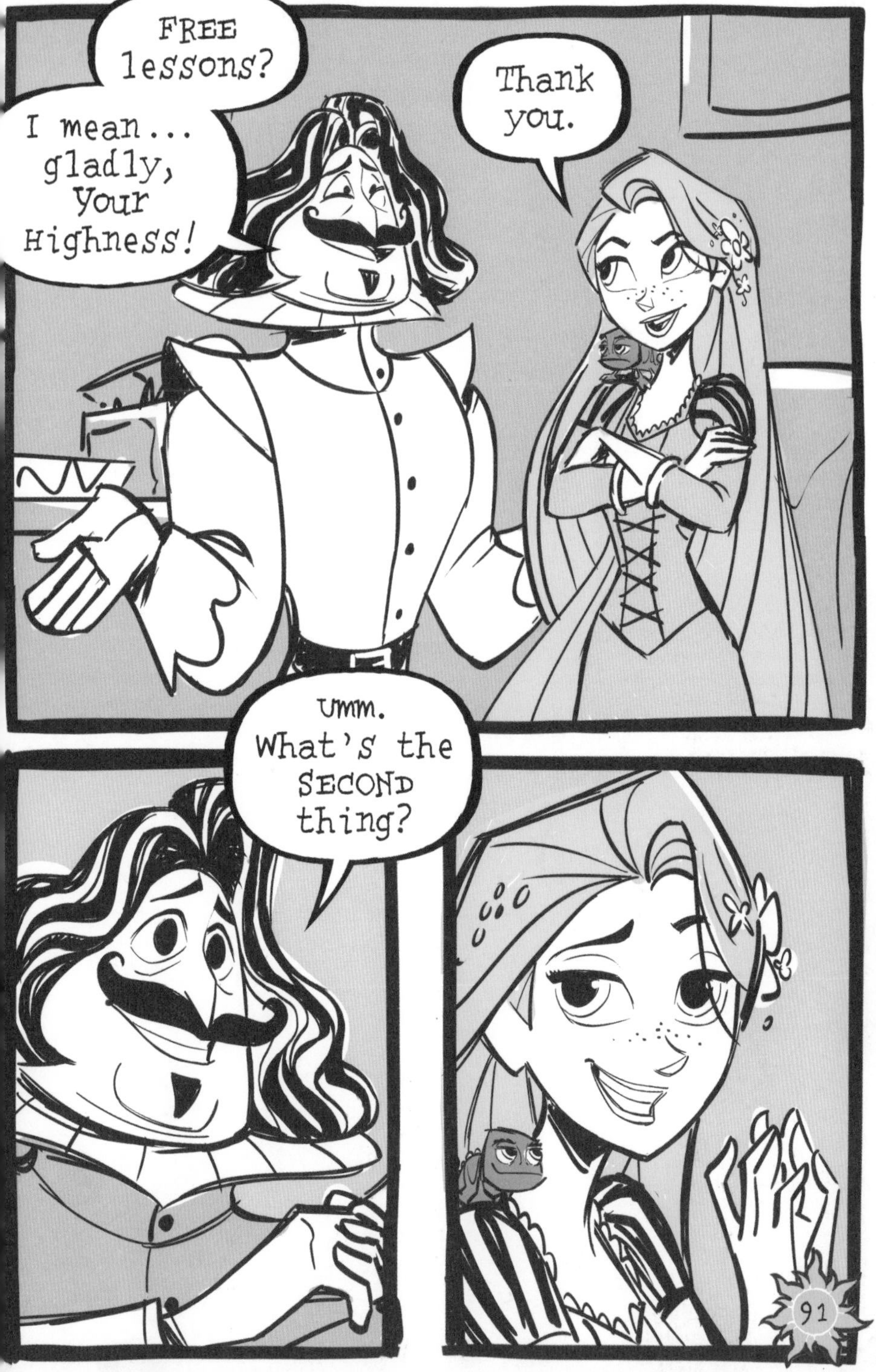
FREE lessons?
I mean... gladly, Your Highness!
Thank you.
Umm. What's the SECOND thing?

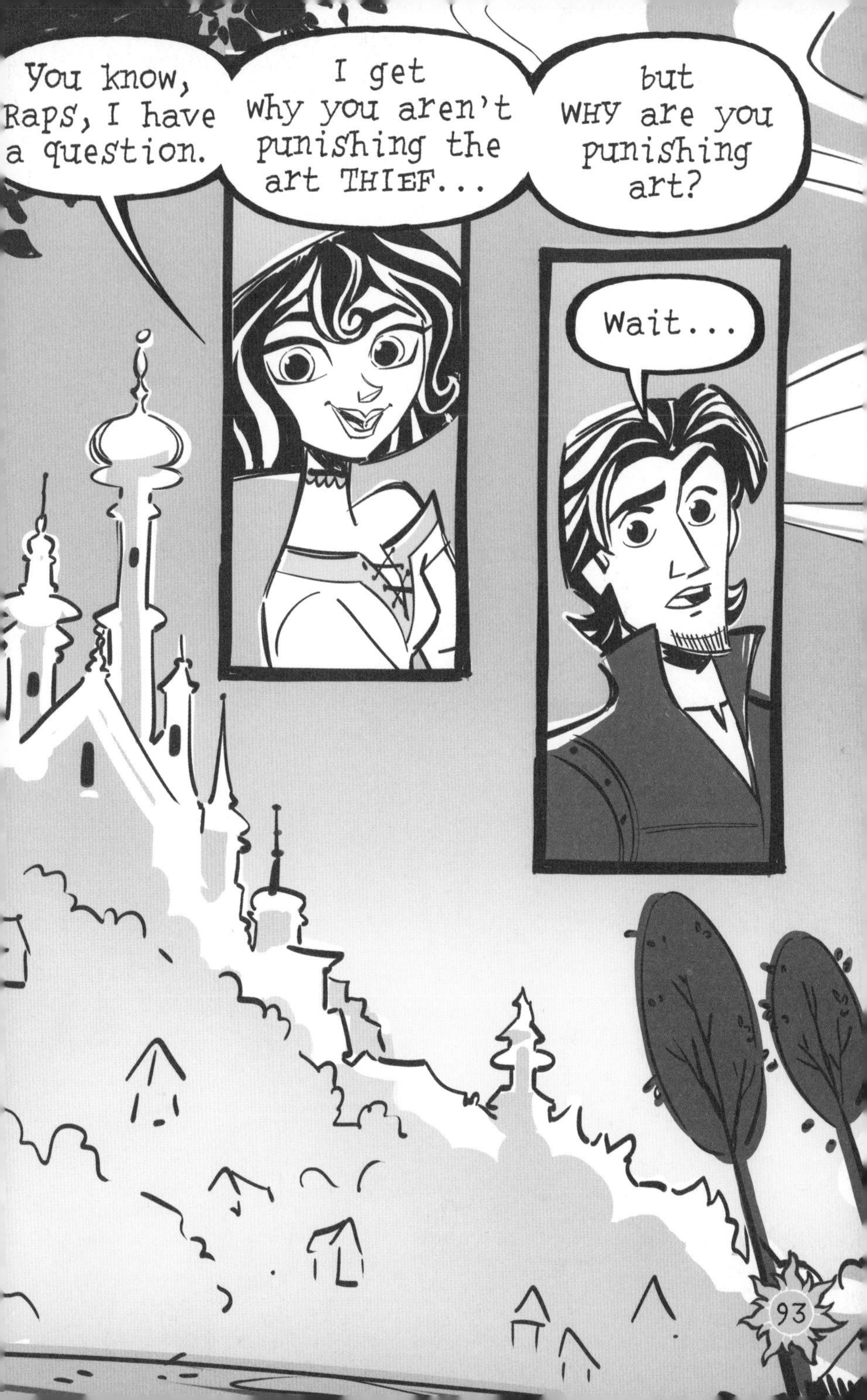

You know, Raps, I have a question.
I get why you aren't punishing the art THIEF...
but WHY are you punishing art?
Wait....

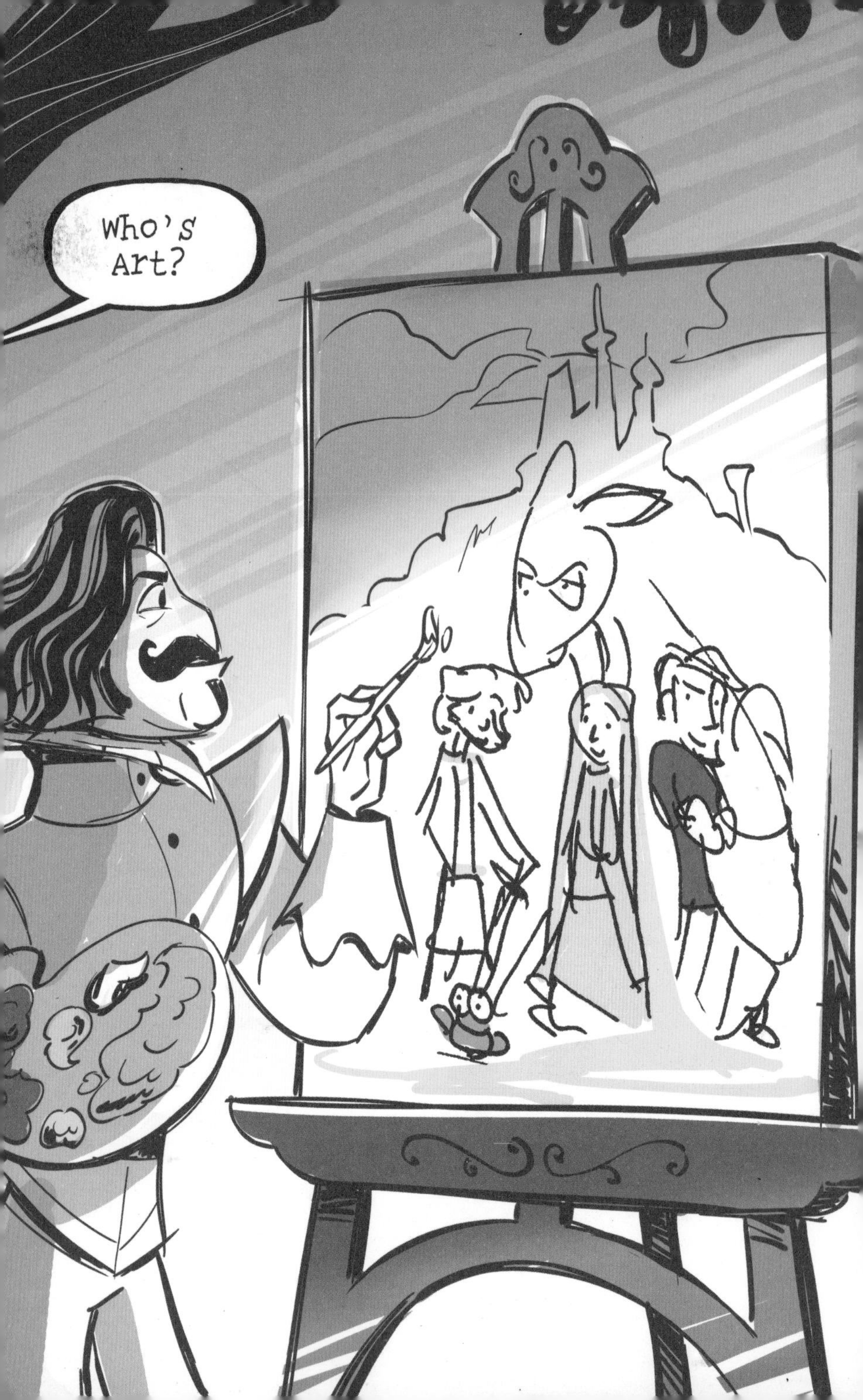
Who's Art?